To Amy
Love Mom
Xmas 2007

"Enjoy"

HIT LIKE A GIRL

BY

STÉPHANIE JULIEN

AuthorHouse™
1663 Liberty Drive, Suite 200
Bloomington, IN 47403
www.authorhouse.com
Phone: 1-800-839-8640

First published by AuthorHouse 9/19/2007

ISBN: 978-1-4343-2970-7 (sc)

Printed in the United States of America
Bloomington, Indiana

This book is printed on acid-free paper.

Chapter 1

They had been walking forever. Amy looked over at her best friend Kyle who was marching ahead like a man on a mission.

"Do you really want to do this?" she questioned. He looked over at her, never even shortening his stride and nodded with a serious look on his face. Amy sighed and continued onward. They had been friends for as long as she could remember. Being the tomboy that she was, she had never liked hanging out with girls who played with dolls, gave each other makeovers, or more recently, had a string of boyfriends. She was perfectly content to take the bus to the nearest field with Kyle and play catch or head down to the lake and go fishing. Although she was invariably good at sports, Kyle unfortunately was not. He tried hard and was always excited to head out to the field with her, but he was definitely not a jock. He had relatively short blond hair that always stood on end and glasses that made his green eyes seem twice as big as they actually were. He was scrawny and shorter than she was, not yet having had any major growth spurt. That was why Amy was so confused.

"There it is!" Kyle exclaimed and hurried the last few feet to the doors of the brown brick building. Amy's brown ponytail swished back and forth as they ran up the brick steps. Amy followed Kyle in and they looked from left to right, hoping to find a sign or some kind of clue to guide them in the right direction. They got a sign alright, just not the written kind. A shout came from down the hall, accompanied by a series of grunts.

"This way." Kyle said, heading towards the noise. When they reached the end of the hallway, they gingerly peered into the room. It was a large enough gymnasium with a hardwood floor and cinderblock walls. Several figures dressed in white with colorful belts were sitting on the ground, stretching, while a few others were doing what appeared to be a complicated series of movements. Two men wearing black belts looked like they were fighting, although they always seemed to know just what the other one was going to do. Amy stood transfixed by the sight with her mouth hanging open, while Kyle grinned like a maniac.

"Did you see that? This is so cool!" he whispered excitedly. The men stopped fighting and one of them came over to speak to them.

"Hello, you're welcome to come in." he said and Amy suddenly became aware that they were still standing in the doorway like idiots. She blushed bright red and hurriedly stepped inside.

"Will you be joining us today?" he inquired and Kyle nodded emphatically.

"Yes, although I'm not sure what we need." Kyle said and the man smiled.

"As long as you have comfortable pants and a t-shirt you'll be fine. You can take off your shoes and socks and leave them over there along with the rest of your stuff. There are change rooms through that door." he said, pointing to an area that was cluttered with flip-flops and running shoes and the door right next to it.

"I'm Charles by the way." the man said. His hair was almost as black as his belt and his eyes were a striking blue. Charles was tall and well built and next to him, Kyle looked like a preschooler.

"I'm Kyle and this is my friend Amy. We don't actually go to this college, but we were still hoping to join the club. Will that be okay?" Kyle asked nervously. One day, out of the blue, Kyle had gotten the idea in his head that he wanted to learn karate. After that, there had been no stopping him. He checked out clubs all over the city and had been very upset to discover that they were all too expensive or too far away. Kyle had been ecstatic when his neighbor had mentioned this club to him. Being a college club, it was a lot more affordable and also somewhat less formal. At Kyle's urging, they had taken the bus across town and unfortunately had gotten off at the wrong end of the campus, hence the long walk.

"That's fine. There are a bunch of us who aren't students at the college, myself included. This is an adult class, but if you think you can handle it, you're in." Charles said amicably.

"Sure we can handle it! We'll go get changed." Kyle said and dragged Amy towards the dressing rooms. She changed as quickly as she could, but Amy wasn't surprised to see Kyle waiting impatiently for her outside the door of the women's change room.

"Hurry, we don't want to be late." he said and they hurried back towards the gym. A short girl in a green belt was in front of them and she surprised them by stopping in the doorway and bowing. Amy was unsure of what to do next, but Kyle just shrugged and followed the girl's lead, bowing quickly in the doorway before moving into the gym. Thankfully, everyone still seemed to be in various stages of warming up. Amy quickly bowed and followed her friend. She and Kyle started stretching their arms and their legs, all the while surveying the crowd. There were maybe twenty people present and the vast majority of them were men. Amy often found herself as a minority since she invariably preferred playing on guys' teams, but this time it was different. Not only was she a girl, but she was the youngest girl at that. Most of the people in the club seemed to be students, although a few of them looked too old to be students unless they had made a career out of studying. Amy mustered as much courage as she could and tried to look like she belonged, even though she and Kyle stood out like a sore thumb in their dark clothes when everyone else was wearing a white uniform.

"Are you nervous?" Amy asked Kyle, leaning in close to whisper in his ear.

"Maybe a little." he conceded, after a moment's hesitation. Just then one of the black belts shouted out a command in Japanese and everyone stopped what they were doing and hurried to the middle of the gym to stand in line. They all seemed to have a designated spot and Amy and Kyle hung back, unsure of what to do. In her limited knowledge of karate, Amy was fairly sure that the black belts were at the top of the food chain. The students had lined up with the black belts at one end and the yellow belts at the other end, followed by one lonely white belt. Figuring the person with the white belt to be the newest recruit, Amy poked Kyle to get his attention and went to stand next to the white belt. Spotting them, the man who appeared to be the instructor walked towards them. The other students all stood stiffly, facing the front with their hands by their sides.

"Ah, new people! Welcome to the club! Just try to follow along with everyone else. Now stand in *Musubi Dachi*, like this, with your hands at your sides." the instructor said, walking back to the front of the class and standing stiffly, with his heels together and his feet turned out at a ninety degree angle from each other. If Kyle was surprised to see that the instructor wasn't Japanese, he didn't show it. Kyle had confided earlier that he was sure the instructor would be a short, slim Japanese man. The man currently standing in front of the class was fairly tall and thickly built with sandy colored hair and Caucasian features. He was definitely not anything like Kyle's dream instructor. He let out a yell and the students bowed in unison. Amy quickly bent over to copy them and out of the corner of her eye, she saw Kyle do the same. After bowing twice to the front of the class, the instructor turned around and the students all bowed to him.

The first part of the class was easy as the instructor lead them through a series of stretches and warm-ups before moving on to harder stuff. That was when it got complicated.

"*Sanchin Dachi Chudan Uke*" the instructor commanded and then he let out a yell and everyone miraculously moved into the same position, answering with a yell of their own. Amy turned helpless eyes to Kyle who shrugged and looked past her to the white belt who had moved his left foot forward at an angle and had produced what appeared to be a block of some kind with his hands. Amy and Kyle spent the rest of the drill attempting to copy the movements of the white belt next to them. It took all of two minutes for Amy to realize that the person with the white belt didn't know much more than they did. She was just starting to get frustrated when the instructor took pity on them.

"*Sensei* Charles, could you please come and help our newcomers?" he said and the man with the black belt that they had met earlier bowed to the instructor and ran over to them. For the rest of the class, they struggled to learn the various kicks, punches and blocks that were presented. Unfortunately, every time they came close to getting one right, the instructor would devise some complicated combination that would throw Amy and Kyle for a loop and leave them completely confused. Poor Kyle was having an especially hard time, since he had never been very coordinated and all the movements required you to do something different with each of your hands at the same time. He made a valiant effort though and by the end of class, he was sweating profusely. Seeing how much he had struggled, Amy was sure that he wouldn't want to come back to another class. They stretched a little, went through the bowing ritual again and then everyone started to leave.

"I didn't get your names. I'm *Sensei* Greg Boltis." the instructor said, coming over to them and extending a sweaty hand.

"Kyle Thompson" Kyle said, eagerly shaking his hand.

"Amy Brendan, it's a pleasure to meet you." Amy said in turn.

"How would I go about getting a uniform?" Kyle asked and Amy's hopes of quitting were quickly dashed.

She could see how karate could be fun she just didn't really enjoy looking like an idiot in front of strangers.

"I can order one for you. You are probably both about a size three. They'll cost around forty dollars." the sensei explained.

"Great." Kyle said and Amy wanted to kick him.

"Should I order a *gi* for each of you then?" Sensei asked, looking at her. Reluctantly, Amy nodded and with a wave the sensei left. There would be no turning back now.

♋

They took the bus back to their neighborhood and got off at the end of the street. The sun was already setting and was casting long shadows in front of them. They lived in Mississauga which was on the outskirts of Toronto. Although it wasn't the worst neighborhood in the city, it was definitely not the safest at night. Amy's mother wasn't big on rules, but she was adamant that Amy not be out alone after dark. Kyle shuffled along next to her. As usual, he wasn't in a hurry to get home. Amy had never actually spent time with Kyle's father, but she knew that he wasn't a nice man. Kyle spent more time at Amy's tiny apartment than he did at his house. His father just didn't seem to care about his only son. Even Kyle's birthdays were spent with Amy and her mother who was very fond of Kyle. She often told Amy that she felt bad for the boy because his dad showed so little interest in him. For that reason, Kyle was always welcome with the Brendans.

"You coming over for supper?" Amy asked casually as she walked along the sidewalk with her hands in her pockets.

"Nah, I think I'll go home and play some computer games for a while. It's getting kinda late." Kyle said, not meeting her gaze. Suddenly, he stopped walking and attempted one of the kicks they had learned in class. Amy tried to think of the name, but she couldn't remember the difficult Japanese term.

"Hiya!" Kyle shouted and followed up his kick with a series of punches. His scrawny arms batting the air looked pretty pitiful and Amy burst out laughing. Kyle turned to her with a silly grin on his face, pulled up one leg and took up a position that made him look like a praying mantis. He scrunched up his face, attempting to look mean and made a hissing sound. Amy doubled over with laughter and soon Kyle joined her.

"We looked pretty pathetic didn't we?" he said between gulps of air.

"We sure did! All my kicks looked exactly the same even though they were supposed to be different and I was pretty much just moving air around with my blocks." Amy said with a final giggle at the memory. Kyle demonstrated his version of one of the blocks and Amy nodded in agreement.

"Exactly!" she said and they both laughed again as they each attempted to recreate the instructor's quick and sharp movement. By then, they had reached Kyle's house and he hesitated on the sidewalk, looking longingly down the street towards Amy's apartment building.

"See ya." he said finally and started up the driveway. The house was small and very rundown. Amy couldn't remember ever seeing Kyle's father outside fixing it up. Kyle was the one who cut the grass in the summer and everything else was left undone. The leaves were never raked, the paint was left to peel and the shutter on the left had been hanging by its last hinge since before Kyle's mother had moved out. And that had been a long time ago. Amy barely remembered Mrs. Thompson. She had been nice enough, but smoked like a chimney and was always coughing up a lung. Amy had always wondered if Mrs. Thompson was sick or if she just liked to sleep a lot, but either way, she always looked a little drowsy and slept most of the day. She had left when Amy and Kyle were in the second grade and they had never seen her again. Amy had asked Kyle before if he missed his mother, but he just shrugged and avoided answering.

Amy arrived in her apartment only five minutes before her mother. She had barely sat down on the couch when the door opened and Maya Brendan breezed in. Her leather jacket was undone and she somehow managed to juggle two folders, her keys, her purse, a bag of Chinese take-out, and a cup of Tim Horton's coffee and still open the door. She kicked the door closed behind her and dropped everything on the kitchen table before plopping down on the couch next to her daughter.

"Hey." she said to her daughter, as she leaned her head back and closed her eyes.

"Hey." Amy said back. Kyle thought her mother was the coolest person in the world and Amy tended to agree. She turned her head to look at her mother. She had long dark hair with reddish highlights and an olive complexion. Her eyes were slightly almond shaped and were huge and dark, making her look exotic. She could be very beautiful if she dressed up, but Maya was very tough and tomboyish like her daughter. She preferred to live in jeans and a sweater when she was at home and almost always wore dark pants with her black leather jacket when she went to work. Maya Brendan was a detective with the Ontario Provincial Police. After spending years in a blocky navy blue uniform, she had graduated to a plain-clothes job and a good one at that. Amy was very proud of her mother, who she knew was good at her job. She also worried about her constantly because if anything ever happened to Maya, Amy would be completely alone. They were all each other had.

"We should eat before the food gets cold." Maya said, getting to her feet and shrugging out of her jacket. Amy followed her mother and they worked as a team, quickly setting the table and dishing out the food. Amy carefully moved the folders off the table and placed them on the counter. She looked at her mother questioningly.

"Work. There's a case that is driving me crazy. I feel like the answer is right in front of my face, but I can't see it." Maya explained as she placed two plates on the table.

"I know what you mean. That's exactly how I feel in math class." Amy said and her mother laughed.

"You are definitely my daughter. I was never good in math." she said as they both settled down at the table. Suddenly, Amy jumped up and ran back to the couch, taking a piece of paper out of her bag.

"Can you sign this?" Amy asked, handing the paper to her mother. Maya eyed Amy questioningly and took the paper from her.

"That depends. What is it?" she asked, unfolding the paper and reading it carefully.

"It's a consent form for me to take karate." Amy explained.

"Since when are you interested in karate?" her mother asked, incredulously.

"I'm not really. It's actually Kyle's idea, but I think it could be fun." Amy answered, honestly. She and her mother were always honest with each other. In some ways, there more like friends or sisters than mother and daughter. Maya started laughing at the thought of scrawny little Kyle doing karate.

"He never does cease to amaze me." Maya said, still chuckling.

"I don't know how long we'll last. We went today and we were awful." Amy said, shaking her head.

"I just can't imagine Kyle doing karate. The poor kid just isn't that coordinated." Maya said and Amy laughed.

"Oh I don't think you could call what he was doing karate." Amy said and stood up to give her mother a quick demonstration. By the time she was done, they were both laughing hard and their plates of food had been pushed away, forgotten.

☙

Kyle stayed in his room all night. He played some computer games and worked on some homework. He dug a chocolate bar and a bag of chips out from under his bed for supper and then went right back to his computer. He watched a ninja movie and researched the history of karate. He was determined to be more prepared for the next karate class. Getting down on his hands and knees, he did push-ups until his arms were aching. He managed seven before collapsing. Dismayed, he rolled over onto his back and started doing sit-ups. After fifteen, he gave up and sat back at his computer, breathing hard. This was going to be harder that he thought. Kyle tensed when he heard banging downstairs and the sound of glass breaking. He held his breath and waited to hear footsteps. When

11

he didn't, he breathed a sigh of relief and reached into his backpack to get the consent form for the karate club. Knowing that his father would never agree to sign the form, Kyle carefully forged his father's signature and put the page back in his bag.

∽

"Yo Thompson! What's your hurry?" a deep voice called. Kyle tried to ignore the voice as he walked across the schoolyard. Suddenly, he was shoved from behind and his glasses went flying as he fell flat on the ground. Without his glasses, Joe Wharton, captain of the football team and the biggest bully in school looked more like a blurry giant than a teenager. He had been hassling Kyle since the ninth grade when Kyle had refused to write an essay for him. Unfortunately, the teacher found out and told the principal who suspended Joe. Kyle had made himself an enemy for life.

"You gonna let your girl fight for you?" Joe taunted and Kyle sensed Amy's presence even though he couldn't quite make out her features. Knowing that Amy would readily fight for him upset Kyle even more. He was tired of being the weak kid and he was counting on karate to help him. He pushed himself to his feet and squared off with the blurry giant.

"Leave her alone Wharton. You know, for a kid who claims to have balls, you sure have a funny way of showing it." Kyle said, trying to sound tough. He knew he was being cocky, but he didn't care. He was angry and tired of being picked on. The punch to the stomach totally caught him off guard and Kyle doubled over in pain, clutching his abdomen. He heard the other kids laughing and felt Amy at his side. Sheepishly, he kept his head down, realizing that he had basically asked for it.

"Do you like those balls Thompson? Or were you looking for bigger ones?" Joe asked mockingly. Kyle ignored him and was glad when they all walked away.

"Are you all right?" Amy asked worriedly, leaning over next to her friend.

"It's cool." Kyle grunted in response and straightened out. Amy handed him his glasses and he put them on, glad that they weren't broken.

"We've gotta get to work." he said, changing the subject. He picked up his backpack and dusted it off before leaving. He walked a few steps before looking back to make sure that Amy was coming with him. With a sigh, she picked up her own backpack, slung it over her shoulder and hurried to catch up with him. Amy was two months older than Kyle. She had never been in a hurry to grow up, but Kyle was. The day he turned sixteen, he had set out to apply for jobs and as usual, Amy had gone with him. They had both gotten jobs at the nearby Canadian Tire store about four months ago and generally worked two or three days a week. Kyle took all the extra shifts he could get and saved all his money. That was the only way he could afford to take karate classes. Now he would have to work a few extra shifts to pay for the uniform, but he was convinced that it would all be worth it one day.

☙

When Amy got home from work that night, she found a note from her mother on the kitchen table saying that she had gotten called back to work and that she probably wouldn't be home until the morning. Amy had no idea how her mother managed to work for days without sleeping and still do a good job. Amy had tried to pull an all-nighter once to finish a project that she had stupidly waited until the last minute to start. It hadn't gone very well. Amy's mother had woken her up early in the morning when she had gotten home from work and they had both worked frantically to finish the project in time for Amy's first period History class. Thinking of that nightmare, Amy pulled out her French book and started to look for quotes for the essay she had been assigned. Although it wasn't due for another week and a half, Amy thought she should probably try starting earlier to see if it made a difference. She had the sneaking suspicion though, that she would still be working on this essay on the night before it was due.

Amy had barely gotten started when there was a knock at the door. She hurried over to the door and peeked through the small hole to see who was there.

"Oh it's you. Come in and you can help me with my math homework." Amy said trying to pretend that she didn't find it odd that Kyle had come over only minutes after she had dropped him off at his house. Kyle didn't say anything as he followed Amy into the living room. He sat down on the couch next to her and held his hands in his lap nervously. Amy wasn't used to seeing him this uptight and she wasn't exactly sure how to handle the situation.

"Is your mom home?" Kyle asked quietly, after a few moments of awkward silence.

"No, she got called back to work." Amy answered, wondering when Kyle was going to tell her what was wrong. Kyle just nodded, but he still wouldn't look at her. After another long, awkward silence, Kyle finally looked over at his friend and cleared his throat.

"My dad….Do you think I could stay here tonight?" Kyle asked. His voice was so low that it was almost a whisper. Amy was totally caught off guard. Although she had suspicions that Kyle's dad might be hurting him, Kyle had never said anything to her. It was like an unspoken rule between them. They just never talked about Kyle's dad or his home life and they never went to his place if they could help it. They either went out or they played video games in Amy's apartment. Amy fought the urge to ask Kyle just what was going on. She knew that if he really wanted to tell her that he would. And she also knew that he wouldn't be asking to stay over unless he really couldn't go home. He had never stayed over before.

"Sure, no problem. My mom probably won't be back until late tomorrow morning anyways." Amy said, trying to sound nonchalant. Relief flooded Kyle's face and Amy beamed, feeling like the best friend in the world. As long as her mother didn't come home and freak, everything would be alright.

"The math homework is really easy. Here, I'll show you." Kyle said eagerly and Amy put all thoughts of her mother out of her mind.

Chapter 2

Kyle felt antsy all day at school. He couldn't wait for school to be over so that he could go back to karate class. When the final bell rang, he hurried to his locker to get his stuff and then met Amy at the front entrance. They caught the bus together and this time made sure to get off at the right stop. They quickly changed and then started stretching.

"You know, when we bow, we bow to the front of the *dojo*. There's usually a shrine there that we are showing respect to." Kyle said, leaning close to Amy as he stretched his left leg. Amy looked over at the front of the class and noticed a picture proudly displayed there.

"Like that?" she asked, pointing it out.

"Kinda. That's probably Master Yamaguchi he's the one who popularized the *GoJu Ryu* style of karate. But it could also be Master Miyagi because he's the one that developed the style. I can't really tell just by the picture." Kyle said knowledgeably. Amy had long since stopped wondering how Kyle knew what he did. He was a wiz at researching on the internet and he often helped Amy with her research for school. Amy had no doubt that Kyle was telling her the truth. When Sensei arrived, he was carrying two plastic bags.

"Here you go. You have time to go put on your new *gi* and you can ask one of the yellow belts to show you how to tie your *obi*." he instructed, handing each of them a uniform.

"Tie our what?" Amy asked, confused.

"Your *obi*. It's your belt." he explained and Amy suddenly felt very stupid.

"Oh sure, thank you." she said and then disappeared into the dressing room. When they came back out a moment later, Amy noticed that Kyle's eyes were sparkling with excitement and she didn't bother to tell him how stupid she thought they both looked in their glorified pajamas. The yellow belts were happy to help them tie their belts. Kyle got it instantly, while it took Amy a few tries to get her knot to look the same as everyone else's. This class started differently than the previous one. It seemed more like a session at the gym than anything else. They did push-ups and sit-ups and something called a squat-kick that forced them to use muscles that Amy didn't even know she had. They jumped rope and ran laps around the gym until Amy and Kyle were sweating buckets into their brand new uniforms.

"We are so going to be sore tomorrow!" Amy complained, through clenched teeth as she forced herself to do another push-up. Kyle didn't answer as he panted next to her. When they were through with that, they were instructed to pair up and work on some drills together. Amy ended up with a tall blue belt girl who seemed nice enough, while Kyle was paired up with a bony brown belt guy who was quick and strong. Amy could practically feel the bruises forming on her forearms as she attempted to block her opponent's strikes. It was even worse with the kicks. She was so afraid of the legs flying at her, that she moved out of the way instead of blocking. Seeing that she was having a hard time, Sensei partnered her up with one of the black belt guys who left her no choice but to block or be run over. Since she wasn't fond of having someone stick his foot right through her abdomen, Amy quickly learned to block the kicks.

Looking over at Kyle, she noticed that he seemed to be doing fairly well with the kicks. His blocks however, weren't quite as good. Amy figured his stomach muscles would be extremely sore in the morning from all the abuse he was taking.

"They say that what doesn't kill you will make you stronger. I think that pretty much sums up karate." the black belt said when he saw Amy flinch. Amy laughed and felt herself lighten up a little.

"Well then I guess to be good at karate you need either a high pain tolerance or a very low IQ because no one else would volunteer to get their ass whipped!" Amy quipped, making the black belt laugh. He had a booming laugh that echoed in the gym and made everyone else smile.

"It's probably a little of both." he said finally before continuing the drill. Amy was thankful when the class finally ended.

"*Seiretsu!*" Sensei yelled and everyone scurried into position as they lined-up. Amy and Kyle hurried to the end of the line and stood with their hands by their sides. They were surprised when Sensei retreated to stand off to the side near the other end of the line. He was joined by Sensei Charles who nodded to the next black belt in line.

"*Seiza!*" the black belt yelled and Sensei quickly dropped down into a formal looking kneeling position. Amy watched as Sensei Charles dropped down next and then was followed by the other students in turn. When the white belt next to her got down on his knees, Amy quickly followed him and turned questioning eyes to Kyle.

"Formal bowing." he whispered and then faced the front with a serious expression on his face.

"*Mokuso!*" the higher belt yelled next and Amy was at a loss for what to do.

"Close your eyes and try to relax. Take deep breaths in through your nose and out through your mouth." Sensei explained and Amy and Kyle complied.

"*Mokuso Naore!*" the black belt said and Amy opened her eyes and was relieved to see that everyone else had opened their eyes as well.

"*Shomen Ni Taishite, Rei!*" he commanded and everyone placed their hands on the ground, one at a time and bowed towards the front of the gym, their foreheads not quite touching the floor.

"*Kaiso Ni Taishite, Rei!*" came the next command and everyone again bowed towards the front. Amy was just starting to get the hang of the ritual when something else surprised her.

"Goju-do!" he yelled.

"Goju-do!" everyone repeated and Amy listened stupidly in silence.

"Should be proud to be studying Goju-do!" he said and again everyone repeated the words.

"Should always observe proper decorum! Should make it our principle to cultivate fortitude and plain spirit! Should cultivate the sense of solidarity on the basis of mutual support! Should be an honorable citizen!" Every statement was repeated with conviction and Amy found her voice becoming stronger and more confident.

"*Sensei Ni Taishite, Rei!*" the black belt yelled next and everyone turned to face the two *sensei* at the far end before bowing.

"*Otagai Ni, Rei!*" he commanded and they again bowed to the front. After that, the bowing seemed to be over, because Sensei started talking.

"The next examination will be November twenty fifth, which is six weeks from now. I encourage everyone below brown belt to examine. There will also be a Karate Ontario tournament in two weeks held here at the College if anyone wants to compete. Even if you are not competing, there will be some really good karate going on and it would be great if at least some of you came out to support your club mates. Anyone who wants to compete should see me after class. There will be another tournament in January down in Guelph for those of you who want to plan ahead. *Tate*, stand up." He said after finishing his speech. Amy knew without a doubt that Kyle would want to take the examination in November. She was also afraid that he would want to compete in at least one of those tournaments. What had she gotten herself into?

✌

Amy was examining her new bruises after work on Saturday when she heard a knock at her bedroom door. A moment later, her mother walked in and came over to her. Amy was surprised to see that her mother had actually dressed up, styled her hair and was wearing jewelry.

"What happened?" Maya asked with a frown, when she saw her daughter's bruises.

21

"Nothing. I just didn't realize there was so much contact in karate." Amy answered and her mother's frown deepened. Amy waved off her concerns and tried instead to change the subject.

"You look pretty. What's the occasion?" Amy asked her mother, pulling down her pant leg to hide the bruises on her leg and crossing her arms to draw attention away from them.

"I thought I always looked pretty." Her mother teased, tossing her hair back over her shoulder.

"Sure mom." Amy said, rolling her eyes as she waited patiently for her mother to answer her.

"James is taking us out for dinner. Kyle's welcome to come if he wants to." Maya said and Amy nodded. James Elliott was Maya's partner at work and had been for three years. Amy had once tried to get them together because she thought that James would make the perfect dad. However, Maya had explained that her relationship with James was like the one Amy had with Kyle. Amy had immediately backed off. She couldn't imagine dating Kyle. He was her best friend. He was almost like a brother to her. Dating him would just be wrong!

"Are you sure you want to do this karate thing? I'm glad you're learning some self-defense, but I'd rather not see you get hurt." Maya said softly, losing her joking tone for a moment.

"It's cool mom. Once I learn how to block properly, I'm sure I'll have less bruises. It's only my first week. It's not like I can get any worse." Amy assured her, standing up and heading for her closet. She could feel her mother's eyes on her, but she forced herself to look at the clothes.

"Well I'll let you change. James is picking us up in about ten minutes. Bring your coat." Maya said, standing up and heading for the door. Amy waited until she was gone, before she breathed a sigh of relief. Although her mother generally let her do what she wanted, Amy and Kyle usually stuck with safe things. Amy was usually more adventurous, while Kyle had always been afraid to try new things. This time it was different. Not only was karate a contact sport, but she was taking the class with adults at a College that was a half hour bus ride from her apartment on a good day. Amy could tell that her mother wasn't thrilled about this, but she also knew that her mother trusted her to make good decisions. That caused a problem, because though Amy wasn't exactly sure that taking Karate was a good idea, she had just begun to realize that it was something that she really wanted to do. And once she had her mind set on something, there was no stopping her.

ॐ

While finishing up his French essay on his computer, Kyle's stomach started to growl. He continued writing however, staunchly refusing to give in to his hunger and wander down to the kitchen. He had seen his father briefly on his way in after work and knew that he would be wise to stay out of his father's way for the night. He managed to finish the paragraph before he heard it.

"KYLE! Get your ass down here!" he heard his father yell. Kyle froze and his heart seemed to stop as he tried to decide what to do. He contemplated ignoring his father or escaping out the window, but finally decided against it. Knowing that it was a bad idea to make his father wait, Kyle finally got up from his chair. His feet felt like lead weights as he walked to the door. Taking a deep breath, he opened the door and stepped out into the hallway. Kyle started down the stairs and could hear his father swearing as he neared the bottom. Kyle closed his eyes and tried to calm himself enough to stop shaking. Finally, he turned towards the kitchen and slowly opened his eyes.

☙

"So what's new and exciting?" James asked as he wiped his mouth with the cloth napkin.

"Amy joined a karate club." Maya said, looking over at Amy to elaborate.

"Really? Well that definitely qualifies as exciting. What made you want to learn karate?" James asked, looking surprised. Amy was seriously starting to get annoyed at everyone for acting so surprised. It wasn't *that* odd for her to want to join karate.

"It seemed pretty cool. Besides it was Kyle's idea. He's the one that really wants to learn." Amy answered finally. Just like her mother had, James started to laugh at that. He knew Kyle pretty well and saw how absurd it was for him to want to attempt something like karate.

"Where is your partner in crime tonight anyways?" James asked with a silly grin on his face.

"Kyle had to work." Amy told him, trying not to sound defensive.

"You know, I've always wanted to learn karate. Maybe you can teach me and your mom some moves once you get really good." James said and Amy relaxed. He sounded truly interested and had lost his mocking tone.

"Sure! And maybe you could come and watch the tournament competitions with us!" Amy said excitedly.

"Sounds like fun, just let me know when." James said agreeably. Even if he would never be her father, it sure was nice to have a cool guy to go on outings with. It was almost as good as the real thing.

He shivered in the cold and glanced around furtively. He was afraid. Kyle had never thought he would end up here. He glanced at his watch for the umpteenth time then shoved his hands deep into his pockets. He cast a wary glance down the long deserted alley and gulped. He could feel sweat beading on his upper lip, but ignored it. The unfamiliar objects in the alley were cast in shadows and Kyle struggled to make them out. He imagined all the awful things that could be hiding in those shadows and shivered again. This time, it wasn't because of the cold. Kyle could feel the money his dad had given him burning a hole in his pocket. Looking the other way, he saw the deserted street. At this time of night, everything was quiet except for the occasional siren or the sound of a taxi passing by. Kyle tried to ignore his fears.

"You're in karate now. You're supposed to be tough." he muttered to himself. He was startled by a noise nearby and started to turn his head to look. He was stopped dead by an arm that suddenly snaked around his neck, holding him in a choke hold. Kyle's breath caught in his throat and he felt his heart drumming in his chest.

"Don't make a sound." a voice hissed in his ear. A moment later, he was released and he stumbled a few steps back, his hands massaging his throat as he gratefully sucked in air. The figure in front of him was wearing a beat-up leather bomber jacket over a grey hooded sweatshirt. Kyle couldn't make out his face. The man took a step forward and held out his hand, clearly wanting Kyle to shake it.

"You had better have the money." he growled in a low voice. Kyle quickly plunged his shaking hand into his back pocket and pulled out the crumpled bills that his father had given him. Stepping cautiously towards the hooded man, Kyle attempted to hand him the money. He was surprised when the man shook his hand, pumping it briskly and then turned around, quickly disappearing into the shadows. Kyle looked down incredulously at his hand and saw that the money had been replaced by a small bag of white powder. Realizing what it was, Kyle quickly stuffed the bag into the pocket of his jeans and looked around, hoping that no one had seen what he had just done. He took a deep breath to try and calm himself. This was not the kind of thing he had ever expected to be doing, but desperate times called for desperate measures.

❧

Maya flopped down in front of the television set after James dropped them off at home. Amy was on her way to her room, when her mother called out to her.

"Hey, there's a good movie playing on TV. Why don't you come and watch it with me?" Maya said and Amy backtracked to the living room.

"What movie?" she asked curiously. Maya tried to hide a grin as she looked up at her daughter.

"Karate Kid." she said and Amy smiled.

"Oh mom!" she exclaimed and playfully punched her mother in the arm. Amy pretended to be annoyed, but she sat down next to her mother anyways and snuggled in close. All through the movie, Amy kept up a running commentary, telling her mother how the strikes, blocks and kicks in the movie were very similar to what she was learning in class.

"So is your sensei anything like Mr. Miyagi?" Maya teased.

"Not at all! I think that's what Kyle was expecting though." Amy answered with a laugh.

"I haven't seen Kyle in days. What's he up to besides karate?" Maya asked her daughter. Amy just shrugged and waited for a moment before answering.

"He says he has a lot of homework, but I think he's just been playing computer games. He knows I think only nerds play computer games." At least that's what she hoped he was doing.

Chapter 3

For the next few weeks, Amy pretty much only saw Kyle at karate. They were enjoying class and breathing heavily when Sensei Charles stopped for a moment to allow everyone to catch their breath.

"Good karate is not just about the techniques. A technique can be great, but if it doesn't have any power behind it, it won't do any good. I want you all to work on putting more energy behind your strikes and I want you to focus your blocks. The Japanese word for energy or spirit is *ki*. You can think of it however you want. Some people regard it as life energy while others, like George Lucas call it 'the Force'." Sensei Charles explained and the students smiled at his analogy.

"Here he goes again." the orange belt next to Amy said, rolling his eyes, but Kyle could tell that he was as eager to hear what Charles had to say as the rest of them were.

"Some believe that a person's *ki* can be so great that it can go beyond the body into a target thus healing or devastating that target without even touching it. You've probably all seen it at least once in a movie or on TV." he continued and Kyle felt himself nodding in agreement.

"We can't measure *ki*, but we can feel it. We can feel it in *kata*, when our movements are strong and sure and everything seems to happen just right or in *kumite* when all our energy pours into a single point of perfect contact. When you experience *ki*, you'll know it." Charles explained, demonstrating with slow, purposeful techniques.

"We all have this energy building up inside us. It's random, loose, wild. To be useful it has to be controlled or concentrated. *Kime* is what the Japanese call the focus of this energy. Think of it as the point at which all of your physical, mental and spiritual energies converge on one spot for one instant. That's *kime*, and that's what makes karate so powerful." Kyle watched his Sensei in awe, not even blinking, drinking in all that he was saying. This was exactly what he needed to learn.

"It's like concentrating all of the sun's rays through a magnifying glass on one spot to burn something. Only in karate, it's done very quickly. The specific point of *kime* is usually where you *kiai*. A *kiai* is not just a random shout. The word actually refers to the concentration of spirit or energy to the point where it can no longer be contained in the body. So it escapes. And the safest way for this release of energy is through the mouth. Trust me, you don't want it to come out anywhere else." Charles said and everyone laughed.

"A real *kiai* is spontaneous. It just comes out on its own. If you have to force it, then it's not real and you're defeating the purpose. I want you all to work on your *kime* and your *kiai* for the rest of the drill. We'll *kiai* on every strike." Charles added before continuing the drill.

Kyle put all his soul and all the energy he could muster into the punches. He was convinced that karate was the solution to his problem and he was going to do everything he could to become the strong capable man that he wanted to be. Someone to be feared. So he wouldn't have to be afraid.

❧

James picked Amy and Kyle up the day of the tournament. Although they wouldn't be competing, they were both very excited to be going, even if it was just to watch. Kyle led the way up in the stands and they settled down to watch. The competition was already in full swing with six rings in use and hundreds of competitors. There were so many people there that it took Kyle and Amy more than ten minutes of searching before they found someone that they knew. It was funny to watch the little kids bouncing around in the ring, spending more time crying because they had gotten hit than actually fighting. The adults were more interesting, especially once the intermediate divisions were announced. Luckily James, Kyle and Amy found themselves seated right in front of the ring where the women's advanced *kumite* competition was being held. There were five women competing, from green to brown belt, and Amy was excited to see what advanced fighting would look like. She cringed inwardly when she saw a delicate-looking girl with long blond hair pulled back into a ponytail. Amy instantly felt bad for the girl, assuming that she would get hit hard by the bigger butch-like girl who also stepped up to the mat. Amy nudged James and pointed out the girl.

"That girl looks super fragile. I'm afraid to see what's going to happen to her." Amy told him with a grimace.

"Don't count her out yet. She just might surprise you." James replied with a knowing look on his face. A few minutes later, Amy understood what he meant. The blond girl was winning and by a lot. Every time the blonde girl kicked her opponent, it made a loud smacking sound that could be heard all the way up the bleachers.

"Whoa! I'm sure glad I don't have to fight her!" Kyle said after a while. He flinched when she whacked the other girl again in the ribs.

"I sure hope that other girl has spare ribs, because she's going to need them by the time they're done this match!" James said and they all laughed, but Amy was secretly pleased that the girl was so good. It gave her hope that maybe she herself could be a good fighter. They shifted their attention to the guys who had started fighting in the next ring and the look on Kyle's face showed Amy just how much the intense fighting made him uneasy. The guys' match was stopped for a bloody nose and they turned back to the girls' ring.

"Hey look! Spare-ribs is in the finals!" Amy exclaimed excitedly. They all watched in fascination as the two brown belt girls competed for the top spot.

"This is exciting!" James said, rubbing his hands together as he darted his eyes back and forth between the two rings. Amy was on the edge of her seat with her fingers and her toes crossed as she cheered on the blond girl. Two minutes later, Amy jumped out of her seat when they announced that the blond girl was the intermediate women's *kumite* champion. The guys weren't nearly as excited as she was, but they both recognized a champion when they saw one.

After watching a few of the black belt matches, they picked up Maya and James took them all out for pizza.

Amy and Kyle told Maya all about the tournament while they sat at the pizza parlour.

"… and then spare-ribs totally finished off the other girl with this wicked kick to the side. It was awesome!" Kyle exclaimed and Maya looked confused.

"Spare-ribs?" she asked, raising her eyebrows.

"You had to be there mom." Amy said waving her off and Maya nodded her understanding.

"Sure thing funny-bone." Maya joked. James laughed and Amy rolled her eyes while it was Kyle's turn to be confused.

"It's a joke Kyle. You know spare-ribs, funny-bone?" Amy tried explaining and although Kyle nodded, she could tell by the blank look on his face that he still didn't get it.

"It's okay Kyle, it'll come to you eventually." Maya said while James choked on his pizza because he was laughing so hard. By the time they had saved James and packed up the left-over pizza, it was time to go. Amy was sad to see the evening end, but the look on Kyle's face said that he was much more disappointed than she was. Amy wondered again what was going on in Kyle's life. Maybe one day, he would trust her enough to tell her. Or maybe she would just have to beat it out of him, one rib at a time.

✂

Kyle never came over for dinner anymore and they rarely hung out. Of all things, Kyle seemed to be ignoring Amy's mother, although Amy had no idea why. Kyle had always liked Maya and had said more than once that he was envious of Amy because her mother was so cool. Now though, Amy was beginning to think that there was something really wrong going on at the Thompson house and she was determined to find out what it was.

Amy decided that she would go over to Kyle's house after the karate belt exam and she would force him to tell her what was going on. She was, after all, bigger than him and knew that she could persuade him to spill his guts. Because she now had a plan, Amy didn't bother Kyle with her usual questions as they rode the bus to the College. Instead, they talked about the exam and tried to guess how it would go. Amy could tell that Kyle was very nervous and she had to admit that she was as well. Amy took her time changing into her *gi*, hoping to calm herself. She tied the ties tightly on her top and made sure that the ends of her belt were the same length. When she was finally satisfied, she went out to meet Kyle. She found him in the gym, working on some kicks. Amy watched him for a few minutes and was surprised to see that his kicks were actually good. Maybe he wasn't as flexible as she was, but he hit his target and Amy could easily distinguish between the four basic types of kicks.

"Looking good! Let's set up and then we can practice some *Yakusoku kumite*." Amy suggested and Kyle quit practicing long enough to follow her. They had arrived very early to class so that they could practice beforehand. However, being the first ones to arrive, they had the added responsibility of sweeping the floor of the *dojo* and taking out all the equipment. They made sure to take everything out of the locker that they could think of, because they didn't know what would be used for the examination. In no time, Amy had piled speed mitts, a bag containing skipping ropes and a duffle bag full of *kumite* mitts in Kyle's arms. The pile was so high that he could barely see over it. Amy slammed the locker shut and picked up the picture of the master and the first aid kit and steered Kyle back to the gym. Since the gym was used by many different people, it was usually dirty. So the lower level belts, usually the white belts or the yellow belts would carefully sweep the floor before each class to make training easier. There was nothing more annoying than training barefoot on a sandy floor. While Kyle ran back and forth across the gym with the giant push broom, Amy set up the picture of the master at the front. She took a step back and bowed to him before relieving Kyle and sweeping the rest of the floor.

Satisfied that the *dojo* was clean and ready for the class, Amy and Kyle paired up to practice *Yakusoku Kumite*, also known as prearranged sparring. They set up in front of each other with one arm's length of distance separating them. Kyle looked at Amy uncertainly and cleared his throat.

"If you punch me in the face and break my glasses, you are going to be in big trouble." Kyle said and Amy laughed.

"If you give me a bloody nose, you are going to be in even bigger trouble." Amy retorted and Kyle seemed to relax. They practiced the drill several times before they felt confident enough to move on to other things. They practiced their *kata*, a traditional pattern of movement that they had been practicing for weeks now. By that time, some of the other students had arrived and they were all either stretching or practicing. A couple of orange belt guys brought in a table from the hallway, along with some chairs and set them up at the front of the *dojo*.

"*Kiotsuke!*" someone yelled, calling everyone to attention. All the students immediately stopped what they were doing.

"Nolin *Sensei Ni*!" he yelled next and everyone turned towards the door to face Sensei Charles. The final command was yelled out and everyone bowed before Charles waved them off and everyone went back to what they were doing. Charles collected the twenty dollar examination fee from everyone who wished to examine and made a list of their name and rank. By now, Amy and Kyle were really getting nervous.

Ten minutes later, they had bowed in the other sensei and were lined up and waiting to begin. They quickly ran through the ceremonial bows and then Sensei ordered them to spread out and get ready to start. There were five black belts seated at the table in the front looking very intimidating as they scratched notes on the pages before them. None of them smiled and Amy tried to avoid looking at them in order to keep her concentration. She refused to let her nerves get the best of her.

Kyle was right next to Amy and he quickly pushed his glasses higher up on his nose before returning his fisted hands to his sides. The lone brown belt in the group was ordered up front where he would be demonstrating all the movements.

"Okay! We are going to start with *Kihon*, basics. Mike will give you a demonstration. You'll do ten on counts and then ten on your own time. Start with *Jodan Tzuki*, upper level punch. *Hajime*! Go ahead!" Sensei explained, nodding to Mike to begin the demonstration. Kyle felt his muscles tense up in anticipation. He was glad they were starting with something easy because it would give him time to lose some of the tension that always made his movements seem more awkward.

Done with basics, they split up according to rank and presented their *Kihon Ido*, basic movements. Kyle found this part more difficult because he found it hard to concentrate on so many things at once. He had to block and move forward in the correct stance and so he had to concentrate on moving his arms and legs at the same time. For someone as uncoordinated as Kyle, this was a huge challenge. When that was finally over, they moved on to *Kata*. As white belts, they had only been taught one *Kata, Taikyoku Jodan Ni* and Kyle was certainly glad for that. After performing just the single *kata*, which lasted all of thirty seconds, Kyle was breathing hard and his muscles were aching. He pitied the blue belts that had to do four *kata*s in a row before earning a rest.

After nearly an hour an a half of hard work, Kyle and Amy finished up their exam requirements, by demonstrating the *Yakusoku Kumite* that they had practiced earlier. They only messed up once, but kept going and Kyle actually thought they had done well. He knew that his techniques weren't perfect. He wasn't as quick as Amy or as crisp as the higher belts, but at least he had been able to perform every strike, kick and block that had been asked of him. He was smiling as he watched the end of the examination for the higher belts. One of their requirements was sparring and Kyle watched in awe as they fought match after match.

"One day, we'll be able to fight like that. You'll see." Kyle vowed, leaning over to whisper in Amy's ear. She smiled at him and nodded, her face still red from the exertion of their own test.

And just like that it was over. Somehow, Kyle had expected their test to be a bigger deal. As if he would walk out of there a stronger man, a force to be reckoned with. He did not expect to have to wait a week before learning the results.

~

Although most of the other students were going out for wings, Amy and Kyle went home. The exam had taken more than two hours and darkness had long since fallen outside. They rode the bus in silence back to their neighborhood and started walking towards home. Amy was strangely quiet and Kyle wondered what she was thinking about. When they arrived at the foot of his driveway, Kyle turned to Amy to say goodbye and was surprised to see her walk right past him towards the house. He felt panic rise within him as he took off after her. The last thing he wanted was for Amy to walk in on his father when he was in a bad mood.

"Amy wait!" he called and reached her just as she was pulling open the door.

"You never come over anymore Kyle. So I am going to come over to your house. We just had our first exam for God's sake! We should be celebrating!" Amy said, exasperated, and pulled open the door. Knowing there was no way he could stop her now, Kyle followed her into the house and quickly looked around for his father. He was relieved when he didn't see him. Unfortunately, Amy didn't just stay in the entrance. She started walking towards the stairs before Kyle could stop her. On the way, she happened to glance in the kitchen and stopped dead. Kyle hurried to her side and reluctantly followed her gaze. The kitchen was a mess. Some of the cupboard doors hung open, while dirty dishes cluttered the counter tops. Seated at the table, were his father and another man who probably weighed several hundred pounds and Kyle was sure most of that weight was muscle. His head was shaved bald and his bare arms were covered with tattoos. Kyle's dad looked as scrawny as his son compared to the giant sitting beside him. His hair was too long and hung in a greasy mess. His clothes were tattered and Kyle could see several holes in his pants and shirt.

The giant noticed them first. He grunted and nodded towards them and Kyle's dad turned towards the doorway. Kyle's dad still had the syringe in his arm from the drugs he had been injecting and the tourniquet around his upper arm held back his rolled-up sleeve. Amy gasped and the giant narrowed his eyes, looking mean and intimidating. Before Kyle could even come up with a plan for damage control, his father had tossed the empty syringe aside and was striding towards them. He grabbed Amy by the arm and used his other hand to pin Kyle to the wall by his neck. He was squeezing so tightly that Kyle could barely breathe. He could see Amy struggling out of the corner of his eye and wished he were as adept as his sensei at karate. Kyle knew that even if he could tackle his father that the giant would surely finish him off. Kyle's dad released him when Amy managed to escape his hold on her. She ran two steps before plowing head-first into the giant. She opened her mouth to scream but he clamped a hand down that covered most of her face. He twisted her arms behind her and shoved her up against the wall.

"If your bitch of a mother comes anywhere near me, I'll kill you both. So you had better keep your pretty little mouth shut. Do you hear me?!" Kyle's father screamed. Amy really thought he would kill her right then and there and she closed her eyes, expecting the worst.

"She won't say anything! I promise Dad, I'll make sure that she doesn't say anything. She understands, trust me!" Kyle said, pleading with his father to leave them alone.

"Her mom's a fucking cop, Kyle! Do you think I'm stupid!" he raged and Amy gulped, daring to open her eyes for a moment. Kyle was standing in front of his father with his hands up in a submissive gesture.

"No! But she won't say anything! She's my friend Dad. She won't get us in trouble!" Kyle tried again and finally his father took one last swing at his son before walking back into the kitchen. Kyle picked himself back up and hurried over to Amy as the giant dropped her back on the floor. He took her by the hand and dragged her up to his room, locking the door behind them. They were both breathing hard and Kyle kept his gaze on the ground, not wanting to know what his best friend thought of him right now. They sat in silence, in the dark for a long while until Kyle finally got the courage to say something.

"You can't tell your mom, Amy." Kyle said quietly and Amy's head snapped up.

"He's doing drugs Kyle! He could have killed us!" Amy exclaimed and Kyle put a finger to his lips to get her to quiet down.

"If you tell your mom she'll have him arrested then what am I going to do?" Kyle asked and Amy sighed.

"I don't know Kyle, but anything's better than this. Don't you think?" Amy said, more quietly this time.

"I'm in on it too Amy. I'm the one who buys most of the drugs. Do you want to get me arrested? Because if your mom arrests my dad, she'll have to arrest me too." Kyle said and Amy gasped.

"But you've never tried any drugs, right?" Amy whispered, sounding totally disgusted. Kyle shook his head vehemently.

"Of course not! But my dad gives me the money and makes me buy the drugs for him. That's illegal Amy. I could go to jail. That's why you can't tell anyone. I'm saving up all my money and I've been hiding it in my room. I'm going to try to make it to the end of the school year and then I'm going to run away. Hopefully, I'll have enough money by then." Kyle explained and Amy's mouth dropped open.

"Why didn't you ever tell me any of this?" Amy asked, incredulous. Kyle rolled his eyes at her and she smiled.

"Okay, fine. I know why you didn't tell me. But you were planning on telling me before you left, weren't you?" Amy asked.

"Of course. You're my best friend. I never could have left without saying goodbye." He responded and Amy nodded.

"I promise to keep your secret for now. But you have to promise that you won't leave without telling me first." Amy pledged solemnly.

"I promise." Kyle said, feeling like a weight had been lifted off his shoulders. Just knowing that Amy would keep his secret made him feel better. He had wanted to tell her for a long time, but hadn't wanted to burden her with his problem or risk her mother finding out. At least now, he only had to avoid her mother. That would be hard, but not nearly as hard as it had been to avoid his best friend.

❧

"Are you sure you don't want to come with me?" Amy asked nervously. It was nearly one o'clock in the morning and Kyle had assured her that it was safe for her to leave. Amy wanted Kyle to come and spend the night at her apartment because she was afraid that his dad would try to hurt him again.

"Don't worry Amy, I'll be fine. He never comes up here anyways." Kyle answered, refusing her offer. He unlocked his door and they crept silently down the stairs. They hurried past the kitchen and Kyle let them out the front door. They stood just outside for a moment and looked at each other.

"Remember your promise Amy." Kyle said and Amy nodded, looking her best friend right in the eye.

"I remember. I'll see you in the morning." Amy said and started to walk away. When she reached the end of the driveway, she turned to look back at her friend, standing alone in front of his dilapidated house. She waved and then turned back around and kept walking.

> ✑

Amy let herself into the apartment as quietly as possible. For once, she actually hoped that her mother had been called in to work. She locked the door and then turned to tiptoe to her bedroom. Noticing that the light was on in the living room, Amy sighed and hesitated, trying to decide what she could possibly tell her mother.

"Where the hell have you been?" Maya said, coming to meet her daughter. Amy grimaced as her mother stalked towards her, knowing that she was in big trouble.

"I was at Kyle's and we fell asleep watching a movie." Amy told her mother, saying the first thing that came to her mind.

"You could have at least called! I was worried sick! James is on his way over here. You're damn lucky that he's the only one I called!" Maya vented, her face a mask of anger.

"I'm sorry mom. I didn't do it on purpose." Amy said, hoping to pacify her mother. Maya marched away from her and flipped open her cell phone. She brushed back her hair anxiously as she spoke into the phone. Then she swore loudly and slammed her phone down on the counter.

"You're lucky he wasn't already here, because you would've had both of us to deal with." Maya told Amy, referring to James. Amy knew James well enough to know that he would definitely not be impressed.

"The next time you decide to stay out this late, you had better have the presence of mind to pick up a phone, because you will be grounded for life." Maya threatened, grabbing Amy by the arm to prove her point. Amy flinched and pulled away, feeling for the first time the battle scars caused by the giant. Maya immediately became suspicious.

"What's wrong with your arm?" she asked her daughter. Amy tried to shrug her off, but Maya was insistent as she pulled off her daughter's coat and rolled up her sleeve. Bruises were already starting to form on Amy's pale arms.

"What happened?" Maya asked again, sounding more concerned.

"I just got hit a few times at karate. It's no big deal." Amy said, thankful that she had a ready excuse. Maya ran her hand lightly over the bruises and tried to absorb what her daughter had told her. Amy was afraid that her mother wouldn't believe her. She was just about to add to her story when Maya abruptly dropped her arm.

"I sure hope you're telling me the truth. We've never lied to each other before and this is definitely not the time to start." Maya said, looking her daughter in the eyes, the way she did when trying to determine the integrity of a witness. Amy squirmed under her mother's intense gaze, but tried not to show her nervousness.

"Go to bed." Maya said finally, turning away from her daughter and heading for her room. Amy sagged with relief once her mother was out of sight. She had thought for sure that her mother would figure out what was really going on. Amy knew this was a small victory, but somehow it felt more like a defeat.

⁊

At karate class a week later, Kyle and Amy stood restlessly in line while their sensei riffled through a stack of certificates. Kyle wiped his sweaty palms on his *gi* pants and kept his eyes glued to his sensei.

Kyle jumped when his name was called and he hurried up front. He bowed to his sensei and shook his hand.

"Kyle did very well during the exam last week and for that reason, I am proud to promote him to tenth *kyu*, yellow belt." Sensei announced to the class. Everyone clapped while Kyle proudly accepted the certificate from Sensei and the yellow belt that was handed to him from Sensei Charles. Kyle bowed again and then hurried back to his position at the end of the line, clutching the precious belt and official looking certificate.

"Amy Brendan" Sensei called and Amy hurried up front.

"Amy also examined last week and showed that she has learned a great deal in the last two months or so. Must be because she has a good teacher." he joked while Amy stood by nervously.

"Anyways, I am proud to promote Amy to tenth *kyu*, first level yellow." Sensei continued and everyone clapped for Amy as she bowed to both senseis, shook their hands and accepted her new yellow belt and certificate. She ran back to Kyle and shot him a victorious smile. Kyle grinned back at his best friend, insanely proud that they had both gotten their yellow belts. Kyle knew logically that not much had changed in the last week, but he felt stronger and more powerful than he ever had before. He felt ready to face the world. More importantly, he felt ready to face his world.

❧

Since Sensei had to leave early, Sensei Charles took over for the rest of the class. They were all too excited about their new belts to do anything that required a high level of concentration. So Charles showed them a few self-defense moves that looked like they could be deadly if performed correctly. Kyle barely touched Amy as they went through the drill because he didn't want to accidentally hurt her. Sensei Charles stopped the class after a while and they all turned to him to hear what he had to say.

"I know most of you take karate because it's good exercise or because you want to learn the more spiritual or cultural side of it or maybe just because it sounds cool, but that's not what karate was meant to be. Karate was developed for one reason and that's self-defense. It's a martial art. We may spend most of our time developing the *art* part of it, but we can't ignore the *martial* side of the equation. People expect *karateka* to have certain abilities. They assume that we can fight and that our abilities increase with our rank. Regardless of how good the kihon or how perfect the kata, an advanced black belt should be able to beat the tar out of someone who wishes them or their loved ones harm. That's just the way it is. A black belt who can't fight is not a traditional black belt and something must have gone wrong in their training somewhere along the line. I'm not promoting violence, but I do want you to understand the power of your techniques and the expectation that comes with them. These techniques are made to incapacitate someone, they aren't just for fun. Try a few more." Charles said. There seemed to be a renewed energy in the dojo, but Kyle felt the pressure of these expectations more than most. He needed these techniques to be deadly. For him, that was the whole point.

ℝ

"So?" Maya asked when her daughter walked into the apartment later that night. She was surprised to see Kyle follow Amy into the kitchen.

"Hey Kyle! I haven't seen you in a while!" Maya exclaimed. She was pleasantly surprised to see her daughter's friend after so much time.

"Hi Maya. What's for supper?" Kyle asked jokingly. Amy's mother had always insisted that he call her by her first name and he had always felt comfortable around her. Maya laughed and motioned towards a pizza box on the counter.

"Well I see you haven't changed much! You're still thinking about your stomach!" Maya said fondly. She tousled Kyle's hair before they all sat down around the kitchen table and dug into the pizza. They ate a few bites before Maya broke the silence.

"Are you going to tell me or what?" she asked impatiently setting down her slice of pizza and crossing her arms over her chest.

"Well we passed of course! How could you ever doubt us mom?" Amy asked pretending to be offended. Maya rolled her eyes at her daughter and glanced over at her friend. Kyle's smile lit up his face and he was totally unable to go along with Amy's charade.

"We're both officially yellow belts! Isn't that awesome!" Kyle exclaimed.

"Definitely!" Maya said and held up her hand for a high five. Kyle slapped her hand and then they both made a fist and touched their fists together. Then Maya did the same with her daughter. Amy had given up being too cool and was ready to celebrate. They chatted while they finished their pizza and then Maya and Amy watched while Kyle greedily scarfed down a fourth and fifth piece of pizza before coming up for air.

"You might as well eat the last piece. There's no point in saving it." Amy said, pushing the box closer to her friend. Although he never talked to her about it, Amy knew that Kyle pretty much had to fend for himself at home. She figured he probably didn't get much to eat and what he did eat was probably junk. She only wished he would come over for dinner more often. Then at least she would know that he had a decent meal.

"We're off to the arcade to celebrate. Wanna come?" Amy asked her mother. Most kids would hate to have their mother tag along, but Maya was actually pretty good at the arcade games and she looked young and hip when she wanted too. Amy had never been ashamed of her mother. They were a team and Amy had never stopped thinking that her mother was cool, probably because she actually was cool. Maya never bugged Amy about stupid things like cleaning her room or going to bed on time. Amy helped with the chores and kept her room fairly neat. If it happened to be a mess, it was probably because Amy was really busy with school, so her mother let it be. If there was a really good movie on TV that just happened to be playing late her mother was usually watching it with her. Then they would both roll out of bed in the morning, complain about how tired they were and agree that the movie had been awesome. That's just the kind of relationship that they had always had. Maya reached for her long black winter jacket and was about to put it on when her phone rang. Amy groaned as she slipped into her winter coat and began pulling on her mitts.

"Brendan" Maya answered authoritatively and her face immediately hardened into a grim expression as she listened to what was being said.

"Where" she said as Amy rolled her eyes at Kyle. Her mother was obviously being called in to work on some big case.

"She's so not coming." Amy whispered to Kyle and he shook his head.

"Nope." he said, knowing the drill as well as his friend.

"Yeah, I'll be right there." Maya said before flipping her phone shut. She looked guilty as she shrugged into her coat and slid her phone into one of the pockets.

"Sorry guys, I'm gonna have to take a rain check on this arcade thing. But I'll drop you off on the way then you won't have to walk." Maya said as she ushered the two teens out of the apartment. She locked the door behind them and in no time, Kyle and Amy were jumping out of the car in front of the arcade.

"Wow, she's in a hurry." Kyle muttered as he buttoned up his coat against the cold. The zipper had broken a long time ago and Kyle didn't want to waste his money on fixing it or buying a new coat.

"Yeah, I'm surprised she didn't have the siren on." Amy said sarcastically.

"Does she really have a siren in her car?" Kyle asked, his eyes wide.

"No, you idiot! I was just joking!" Amy exclaimed, throwing her hands up.

"Well you never know! She drives her car for work a lot, she could've had a siren!" Kyle defended himself. Amy just shook her head. She never could believe how someone so smart could say things that were so stupid. Entering the arcade, Kyle made a beeline for the pinball machine in the back corner. It had always been his favorite. Amy watched as he got such a high score on his first round that he won a free game. He was just about to launch another ball when he was rudely shoved to the side.

"What the..!" he muttered and looked up angrily. Joe Wharton had taken his place at the controls with his large hands completely covering the buttons.

"Back off Joe! We were here first!" Amy stated, glaring at the teen. He ignored her completely and tossed a satisfied glance at Kyle.

"Like you're actually going to do something about it." he taunted, his evil grin making Kyle see red. Kyle was about to light into his enemy when Joe's three rather large friends materialized at his side. A glance in the other direction showed that the manager of the arcade was watching them with a frown on his face.

"Let's go Amy." Kyle said and he saw his friend's jaw drop.

"But, Kyle..." she sputtered. Kyle marched away from the pinball table and he heard Amy sigh in frustration and follow him. He could hear her footsteps as she stomped after him.

"I really hate that guy!" she exclaimed as they exited the arcade.

"So do I." Kyle said evenly. He could feel the anger building up in him and he knew that if he had spent one more second in that place, that he would have been forced to act. Kyle was afraid of what would happen if he failed to control himself.

෪

Maya arrived at the crime scene and stepped out of her car. There were three cruisers parked haphazardly in the street and yellow crime scene tape blocked off the area around the apartment building. All the action had drawn out a few curious people, but crime in this area of downtown Toronto wasn't all that unusual and most people just kept walking. Maya walked up to the officer guarding the perimeter and flashed her badge. He nodded and held up the crime scene tape for her to pass under. James met her at the door. He saw the scowl on Maya's face and grinned.

"Crappy timing, as usual." she muttered and James smirked at her.

"Let me guess, you and Amy were having a great time consoling Kyle for failing his karate exam." James said and Maya cracked a smile.

"Actually, we were going out to celebrate because they both passed their exams." Maya said and held out her hand, palm up. They had been climbing the stairs to the second floor and James waited until they had reached the landing before commenting.

"Both of them?" he asked with a grimace. Maya gave a self-satisfied nod. Now it was her partner's turn to scowl as he reached into his pocket and pulled out some money. He handed a five dollar bill to Maya and she placed it in her pocket with a smile.

"I told you he would pass." She said and James waved her off.

"Yeah, yeah." He muttered as he led the way to an apartment at the end of the hall. They entered the apartment and Maya walked straight over to the body that was lying on the ground. She was taken aback by the youthful face that stared up at her with unblinking eyes.

"Her name is Gabriella Fabiolo and she's nineteen years old. She's a journalism student at Ryerson in her second year. Her parents live in Sault-Ste Marie. They've already been contacted and they're on their way." James said, reading off his notepad. Maya surveyed the body with practiced eyes. There was extensive bruising that appeared on the victim's arms and Maya suspected that she would find much more bruising hidden under the girl's clothes. There were also finger marks bruised into the girl's neck and blood on her face that looked like it could have come from a recently broken nose.

"Do we know the cause of death?" Maya asked, glancing up at James.

"Nothing apparent. We'll have to wait for the ME's report, but it looks to me like someone beat her to death." James suggested.

"We'll have to question the parents as soon as they get here to see if she had any enemies. First thing on Monday morning we'll have to head over to the school and interview her friends and classmates." Maya said thoughtfully, already forming a plan of attack. She stood up quickly and turned her back to the corpse.

"We should start by interviewing the other tenants." Maya called over her shoulder as she strode to the door. She had been doing this job long enough to have become fairly comfortable with the corpses. This time however was different. She wasn't sure if it was the age of the victim or the bruises covering her body, but this girl made her think of Amy and Maya had to get away or she wouldn't be able to do her job.

❧

Maya worked most of the weekend and she was already gone Monday morning when Amy woke up. She walked to school with Kyle and they speculated as to what kind of case Maya and James were working. After writing a test in math class, reading several chapters from a book in French class and constructing human pyramids in gym, Amy met Kyle at his locker. She quickly grabbed her coat and dropped her books on the shelf before slamming the door shut and locking it. Kyle was already making his way down the hall and Amy had to hurry to keep up with him. They exited the school and Kyle raced down the steps.

"Let's go Amy! We're going to miss the bus!" Kyle called over his shoulder, slowing down only long enough to glance over his shoulder to see if Amy was coming. In the next moment, he was laying face first on the ground. Kyle lay there, stunned for a moment, until he heard the laugh. He recognized Joe Wharton's laugh before he saw him. Kyle pushed himself up and lunged towards his enemy. He threw a punch before even thinking about it and his fist bounced harmlessly off Joe's thick chest. Joe's puffy black down-filled jacket was unfortunately insulating him against more than just the cold. Joe shoved Kyle back so hard that he went flying backwards. Joe's two faithful thugs caught Kyle and each held onto one of his arms, effectively holding him. Joe took his time sauntering closer while Kyle struggled against his captors.

"I don't know if anyone has ever told you this Thompson, but you hit like a girl." Joe said, his arms crossed over his chest and a smug look on his face. His jeans hung below his hips and Kyle eyed his beige boots warily, praying that they weren't steel toe boots. Joe pushed up his sleeves and cracked his knuckles before balling his hands into fists. Kyle gulped and struggled harder, desperate to get free. Before Joe could make a move, Amy stepped between him and Kyle, standing with her hands on her hips while she glared at Joe. He seemed amused as he looked at her with raised eyebrows.

"Don't!" Kyle said, but Amy ignored him.

"What's the matter Thompson? Are you afraid I'm going to hit your girl?" Joe asked, looking around Amy to watch Kyle squirm. Amy stepped back into the fighting stance that she had learned in karate class and Joe laughed, clearly not afraid of Amy in the least.

"No, he's afraid I'm going to hit you..." Amy said. Lightning fast, she stepped forward and punched Joe in the face. His head snapped back and he staggered backwards a few steps.

"Like a girl." Amy finished watching unfeeling, as Joe cupped his nose with his hands. Kyle seized the moment and elbowed one of the guys hard in the gut. Both teens released him and the taller one pulled back a fist to strike him. Kyle's arm rose automatically as he blocked the punch. Both boys looked at each other, stunned, unable to believe that Kyle had successfully blocked the strike. Recovering quickly, Kyle wound up and smashed his attacker in the face. As the boy backed away, holding his jaw, Kyle felt someone grip his shoulder and he spun around, ready to attack. He stopped short however when he saw who it was. And Principal Edward Bernard did not look happy.

Chapter 4

Maya sat on her desk at work as she discussed the case with a couple of co-workers. James was standing across from her with his arms crossed as he leaned against a filing cabinet. They had canvassed the school during the day and although they had learned a lot about Gabriella Fabiolo, they still didn't have any suspects.

"Brendan, Elliott, get in here!" their captain hollered and Maya got down off her desk and followed James into the boss's office. The office was small and dark and seemed crowded with the three of them inside.

"Where are you with the Fabiolo case?" he asked, not wasting any time.

"We spoke to most of her friends and classmates and we learned that she was active in many sports and that she liked to run in the morning. She also worked at a nearby Tim Horton's and we're going to head over there later to talk to her co-workers. She seemed to have many acquaintances, but not very many good friends. We don't have any suspects so far, but there are still a few people that we need to track down." James answered and Maya nodded in agreement.

"The media is already involved in this case because she was a student, so I want it solved as soon as possible. Table all of your other cases for now. I want this one to be your priority." the captain ordered and Maya nodded again.

"Yes sir." James answered, just as Maya's cell phone rang. She pulled out her phone and turned her back to the men who were still talking.

"Brendan." she said into the phone and listened intently. She blew out a frustrated breath as she heard what the caller was saying.

"You have got to be kidding me!" she said and James looked over, his interest piqued.

"I'm on my way." Maya said and then closed her phone. Both men were waiting curiously when she turned to look at them.

"Problem?" James asked and Maya nodded.

"It was Amy's school. The principal wants to talk to me because Amy and Kyle got in a fight with some other kids." Maya said, sounding thoroughly annoyed.

"Is she alright?" the captain asked.

"Oh she's fine, but she gave the other guy a bloody nose. That's why they want to talk to me." Maya answered. James burst out laughing and the captain chuckled along with him.

"This is so not funny." Maya said, irritated.

"Oh come on Maya, your daughter beat up a boy. You should be proud." James told her and Maya finally cracked a smile.

"I'll bet that boy is embarrassed enough that he'll steer clear of her for the rest of the year." James added grabbing his coat off the back of his chair as he followed Maya through their office on the way to her car.

"Where do you think you're going?" she asked as she opened the driver's side door and got in.

"I really have to see this for myself." James said, slipping into the passenger seat with a grin on his face. Maya sighed and turned the key in the ignition, not wanting to argue.

"Fine, but you have to remember that she is in big trouble for this. Don't go congratulating her or anything." Maya ordered, but James ignored her as he looked out the window.

"Maybe she likes this kid and was just trying to get his attention." he said suddenly and Maya frowned as she looked at him.

"You can't be serious." Maya said evenly.

"It was just a thought." James said with a shrug, obviously trying to hide a smile. Maya rolled her eyes and concentrated on her driving. Sometimes she wondered how she had ended up with three kids instead of just one.

❧

They sat with their hands clasped in their laps, in straight-backed chairs facing his desk. The principal directed his comments at Maya, acting as if Amy wasn't even there.

"You are aware that we have a zero tolerance policy for violence. This would require all the children involved to be suspended. However, since Amy has never been in trouble before, I might consider being a little more lenient." Principal Bernard said seriously. His voice was nasally and he wore a stuffy old suit that looked like it was older that Maya's mother. Maya nodded in agreement, not sure if he was waiting for her to say something or if he was trying to catch his breath. She was starting to get worried that the old coot would keel over right in front of her. How someone this old could run a school full of teenagers was beyond her.

"I feel I must stress the severity of her offence. The boy's nose was bleeding profusely and could easily have been broken. That is not something we take lightly." he continued and Maya glanced over at her daughter, unable to believe that her little girl had almost broken a boy's nose.

"I can assure you that I do see how serious this is and I will make sure that it doesn't happen again." Maya told the principal, resisting the urge to look at her watch. She knew that James was in the car waiting for her and that her captain expected them to get back to work as soon as possible.

"Very well, I will expect to see Amy in detention for the rest of the week." Mr. Bernard said, dismissing them. Maya ushered a sullen Amy out of the office and saw Kyle sitting with his head in his hands in the waiting area. She looked around, but didn't see his father anywhere. Of course, she really didn't expect to. Ken Thompson didn't care about his son enough to even bother coming to meet with the principal. With a sigh, Maya paused in the waiting area. Amy looked at her questioningly, knowing that her mother was anxious to get back to work.

"Go wait in the car. I'll be right out." Maya said and then turned back towards the office. She knocked on the open door and then walked in. Mr. Bernard was looking at her expectantly.

"Mr. Bernard, I was wondering if I could talk to you for a moment about Kyle Thompson." Maya explained.

"Of course, please come in." he said, sounding surprised. Maya closed the door behind her and took a few steps forward. Remembering that she was in a hurry, she remained standing, but took a few steps closer to the desk.

"The Thompsons have been our neighbors for almost eleven years and Amy and Kyle have been friends for almost as long. I know Mr. Thompson fairly well and frankly, it doesn't surprise me that he isn't here. I doubt very much that he would come in, even if you could reach him…which I assume you haven't." Maya stated and the principal listened intently, looking slightly confused as to where she was going with her tirade.

"I'm just saying that if you keep Kyle here until you speak with his father, you might have to keep him here indefinitely. I would gladly act in his father's place and take Kyle home with me." Maya offered and Mr. Bernard frowned.

"Now I understand what you're saying, but I simply cannot discuss a child with someone who is not his guardian. Kyle will wait here until his father comes by." the principal said, looking back down at his papers as if to signify that the conversation was over. Angered by the principal's lack of understanding, Maya took another step forward and tried again.

"Sir, I'm the one who celebrates Kyle's birthday and takes him school shopping. He spends Christmas, Easter and Thanksgiving at my house and he has my number down as an emergency contact for his job. If anyone should be sitting here with him, it's me." Maya explained, leaning forward and resting a hand on the desk. The elderly principal seemed taken aback by her forcefulness and nervously adjusted his wire-rimmed glasses on his beak-like nose.

"Well I suppose I could make an exception, since Kyle's seems to be such a special…case. You've already heard what I said to Amy and the same goes for Kyle. Detention all week and if it happens again they'll be looking at suspension or even expulsion." Mr. Bernard conceded, leaning back in his chair as if to get far away from Maya. Her daughter had told her once that she was intimidating when she went into "cop mode". At the time, it had made her laugh, but now she was glad. It seemed to have helped her get her way with the stuffy old principal.

"Thank you Mr. Bernard." she said and turned to leave.

"H-have a nice day." He stammered, reaching up to adjust his tie and looking very glad to see her go. Maya strode out of the principal's office feeling very pleased with herself. She motioned to Kyle to get up and he nervously approached her. He was very pale and looked scared to death. She wondered if he was afraid of her, the principal, or his father.

"I sprung you. Let's go, we'll talk about this later." Maya said, placing a hand on Kyle's thin shoulder and pushing him ahead of her. He looked over at her curiously, as if making sure that she was telling the truth. Color slowly returned to his face and he sagged with relief.

"Thank you so much Maya. I owe you one." he said, trying to make light of the situation. Maya could tell however that she had saved him from something that he thought would have been horrible. She wanted to ask him about it, but decided that they already had enough serious things to discuss. Discipline and tenderness were not Maya's strong suits. She had always been much better at entertaining the kids than anything else. This time however, there was no getting out of it. She would have to act like the tough mean mother, times two. And James wasn't helping in the least. He had slid over into the driver's side and Amy was in the backseat. As soon as Kyle slipped in beside her, James stuck out his hand, palm out for Kyle to slap.

"Way to go buddy!" he said and Kyle beamed. His smile left his face quickly when he saw Maya glaring at him and James.

"Don't congratulate them! They are both in big trouble. This is so not a good thing and I think they both know that." Maya said, looking from one teen to the other. When she turned to face the front, Amy talked to Kyle in a low voice.

"So, what's the verdict?" she asked and Kyle shrugged.

"Detention for a week." Maya filled in and Kyle groaned, but didn't complain. They were silent the rest of the way home, but Maya could tell that they were far from repentant.

☙

After they had dropped Kyle off at his house, Maya left Amy at the apartment and she and James went back to work.

"We'll talk when I get home. Don't go anywhere." Maya told her daughter strictly before walking out the door. Amy rolled her eyes and made a face at her mother's back before flopping down on the couch and picking up the phone. She dialed Kyle's number and waited for him to pick up.

"Hey." he answered and Amy absently twisted the telephone cord around her fingers.

"So was it worth detention?" Amy asked and Kyle didn't even hesitate before answering.

"Oh yeah! Did you see Joe's face? You totally decked him! It was awesome!" Kyle exclaimed and Amy laughed.

"Yeah, it was pretty cool. You sure messed up those two guys. How does it feel to be macho?" Amy asked and it was Kyle's turn to chuckle.

"Great! Now I can't wait to get back to karate. It really sucks that we have to stay after school for detention because we'll be late for karate class for sure." Kyle complained.

"That's true. Oh well, it was worth it." Amy said and she could hear yelling through the phone.

"I gotta go. I'll talk to you later." Kyle said and abruptly hung up. Amy sat holding the phone and wondered what had just happened. She knew that anything involving Kyle's father had to be bad. She just hoped that Kyle would be okay.

જ

Kyle stepped off the bus and walked down the street. The pavement was slick from the rain that was supposed to freeze overnight. Kyle stuffed his hands in the pockets of his coat and kept his head low to try and keep warm. The cold December wind seemed to slice through him and he could see snowflakes begin to fall in the glow of the streetlights. He nervously looked around as he headed to the spot. The dark alleys looked ominous and Kyle tried to ignore them as he walked past. As he slowed to a stop, he could see a hooded figure walking towards him. He concentrated on the person, wondering if it was going to be the same guy or someone different. Kyle frowned when he saw the man turn suddenly and head down an alley. He was about to cry out when he heard a noise behind him. Kyle whirled around and saw a cop standing a few meters away with his hand near his gun.

"What are you doing out here, son?" the cop asked and Kyle felt himself start to sweat. He was terrified that he would get caught and felt as if he had 'GUILTY' stamped across his forehead. The cop took another step forward and Kyle was able to make out dark eyes and the beginnings of a beard.

"I-I was just walking home." Kyle stammered, taking his hands out of his pockets and trying to look as innocent and inoffensive as possible. The cop seemed to think about his answer before taking his hand away from his gun.

"This is not a safe neighborhood to be walking through. Do you live far from here?" he asked.

"Far enough. I usually take the bus, but I thought it might be good exercise to walk." Kyle said, praying that the cop would stop talking and get in his car so that Kyle could get the drugs for his dad.

"Well you might want to rethink that. Have a good night." the cop said, pulling his hat lower on his head and finally turning back towards his car. He looked back once and Kyle waved before he turned on his heel and started walking away. His heart was still pounding in his chest and he could practically hear his blood whooshing through his arteries. It took all his self control not to look back and eventually he turned onto the next street and stopped. He leaned against the side of the building and tried to catch his breath and calm down.

"That was way too close." he muttered and took off his glasses before running a hand over his face. Before he could put his glasses back on, they were knocked out of his hand and he heard them fall to the pavement. A hand gripped his throat and pinned him to the brick wall. Although Kyle couldn't see clear enough to tell for sure, he just knew that it was the drug dealer.

"You almost got me busted man! You ever let them pigs get that close again and you'll have big problems! You hear me?" the man growled in Kyle's ear and Kyle tried to nod because he was unable to make a sound. He felt the man reach into his coat pockets and when he came up empty, he plunged his hand into Kyle's pant pockets. Kyle felt as though he was being violated and racked his brain, trying to think of an appropriate karate move that might help him. Unfortunately, his beginner's knowledge of karate was a poor match for a gang banger with a gun. Kyle was abruptly released and the man walked away, disappearing in the shadows before Kyle could do anything. He tentatively reached into his pant pockets, looking for the money that his father had given him. When he came up empty, Kyle started to panic and he hurriedly checked his other pockets. He breathed a sigh of relief when he found a small baggie thrust deep into his coat pocket. He didn't even have to look at it to know what it was. Feeling lucky for the third time that day, Kyle crouched down and started to look for his glasses. He felt around gingerly, the dark and his bad eyesight making it impossible for him to make out the glasses. After a few moments of searching, Kyle finally found the glasses and put them on. He almost cried with relief when he saw that they weren't even broken. Kyle had never been a lucky person and it seemed that this day would go down in the record books as being his most lucky day ever.

Taking off his glasses, he wiped them clean with the hem of his shirt and put them back on, still amazed that they were intact. Not wanting to press his luck, he hurried towards the next bus stop, anxious to get home.

ை

Reading the last chapter of her book, Amy lay in her bed that night. Although it was actually much earlier than she usually went to bed, Amy was hoping to be asleep by the time her mother got home so that she could avoid the promised discussion. When she heard the front door open, Amy quickly turned out the light and shut her eyes, pretending to be asleep. A few minutes later, her bedroom door opened and she opened one eye to see her mother's silhouette in the light streaming in from the hallway. She squeezed her eyes shut tightly and tried to keep her breathing even. Opening the door wider, Maya walked in and stopped in front of the bed.

"Nice try Amy, but I know you're not sleeping." Maya said, reaching over to turn on the lamp beside her daughter's bed. Amy sighed and sat up in bed, squinting in the bright light. Maya pulled Amy's desk chair closer to the bed and sat down facing her daughter. She crossed her arms over her chest and stared at Amy.

"So, what happened today? You get your yellow belt and then you go all Rocky on me. What's that about?" she asked and Amy shrugged.

"Joe was about to hit Kyle so I hit him first." She said matter-of-factly.

"Amy, you can't just go around hitting people. I'm sure your karate instructor told you that you are not supposed to use your karate on others." Maya said and Amy rolled her eyes.

"It's not like I just hit him for fun mom. His two friends were holding Kyle so he couldn't defend himself. I had to help him." Amy clarified.

"Of course, but there are other ways. Violence is never the answer. I don't know how many times I've told you that. I see kids in trouble all the time because they resorted to violence without even looking for other alternatives." Maya lectured and Amy sat up straighter in her bed.

"Oh come on mom! Stop treating me like one of your cases. It was one little punch. It's not like you've never done it." Amy said loudly. Maya's eyes widened and she stared at her daughter.

"Yeah sure, I'm such a bad-ass." Maya said sarcastically.

"I seem to remember you elbowing one of your suspects in the face." Amy said, crossing her arms and leaning back against her headboard.

"I didn't have much of a choice. He was a kidnapper and a murderer and he charged at me. There wasn't much else I could do." Maya said, defending her actions.

"Well, there wasn't much else I could do either." Amy said, with a satisfactory grin. Maya blew out a breath and stood up.

"It's not the same thing Amy. What you did was wrong. He's just a kid." Maya stressed and Amy's mouth gaped open.

"You've got to be kidding! This kid is twice Kyle's size and he's always picking on him! You are not going to convince me that it was wrong." Amy said stubbornly and Maya rubbed her eyes wearily.

"I want you to promise me that you won't do it again. You can't afford to be expelled over something like this and the principal already warned you." Maya said, trying to come to some kind of an understanding with her headstrong daughter.

"I can't promise you that mom, not without lying to you." Amy said honestly and Maya put her hands on her hips, shaking her head. Amy had never given her this much trouble before. They were always honest with each other and Maya had rarely had to punish her daughter. Amy usually realized her mistake and did what she had to do to rectify the situation. This time however, the teenager wasn't budging and she was really testing her mother's limits.

"Fine then. You're grounded. No karate and no going out for two weeks." Maya said, calmly replacing the desk chair. Amy stared at her mother incredulously before letting her anger boil over.

"You can't do that! That is so not fair!" Amy shouted as Maya walked to the door of the room.

"I'm the mother, so yes, I can." Maya said evenly and then walked out of the room.

"I can't believe you're doing this! You really suck, you know that?" Amy accused angrily jumping out of bed and following her mother. Maya just shrugged, but didn't turn around.

"You're still grounded." Maya said, turning into her bedroom and shutting the door behind her. She heard Amy cry out in frustration before slamming her own door shut. Maya sighed and sat on her bed. It seemed that the teenage rebellion was finally starting.

ॐ

Amy caught up with Kyle in detention the next day and told him the news.

"No karate for two weeks! She wouldn't do that!" Kyle protested.

"Well, she did. So I guess you'll have to go to karate class by yourself." Amy said, glumly. She sat down at one of the desks and Kyle sat next to her.

"Maybe if you talk to her she'll change her mind." Kyle suggested, leaning into the aisle so that Amy could hear him.

"I tried, she's not budging." she replied and Kyle frowned as he pulled out his notebook.

"This really sucks Amy." he mumbled and started doing his homework.

"Tell me about it." she answered, rolling her eyes. They worked in silence for a while before Kyle leaned over again.

"You should ask James if…" he whispered but was cut off by the teacher.

"No talking!" he bellowed and Kyle rolled his eyes and picked up his pen. Amy sighed and continued with her work, knowing that her mother wouldn't budge. As cool as Maya was, she was also very stubborn and opinionated. When Amy was on her mother's good side she admired these traits, but they definitely didn't work in her favor in times like these.

❧

The following Monday, Kyle went to karate class alone while Amy went to work. She had decided that she would rather be at work than at home with her mother, so she had picked up an extra shift. Amy and Maya had barely spoken since their initial argument. Amy had inherited the stubborn trait from her mother and neither woman was willing to give in and admit that they were wrong. Kyle shook his head at them, knowing that he wouldn't let a little problem like that get between him and someone he cared about. However, it seemed the only people he cared about were Amy and her mother which struck him as odd considering that they weren't even related to him.

After changing into his karate *gi*, he entered the dojo and ambled over to a group of people who were talking.

"Hey Kyle! I haven't seen you in a while. Where's your friend?" Charles asked him when Kyle sidled up next to the black belt.

"She's grounded." Kyle said and a few of the other people snickered.

"What did she do to get grounded?" Dave asked with a smirk on his face.

"Some guys picked a fight with us at school and she punched one of them in the face and gave him a bloody nose." Kyle explained and they all started to laugh.

"That's awesome!" Dave exclaimed, doubling over with laughter. Charles had an odd look on his face so Kyle hurried to explain.

"Two guys were holding me back and the other one was about to hit me, but Amy got in front of him and hit him first. She gave him plenty of warning, but he didn't seem to be afraid of her." Kyle said and Charles chuckled.

"Big mistake." he muttered and Kyle nodded.

"This guy has been harassing us for a long time and I think he might finally take the hint and back off." Kyle added and everyone nodded.

"Well, at least you followed some of Master Miyagi's three basic rules: do not strike others, do not be struck by others and avoid trouble at all costs." Charles dictated and the others nodded in agreement.

"Leave it to you to know all the quotes by heart." Dave chuckled and Charles shrugged before telling everyone to line up and beginning the class.

❧

Maya zipped up her coat against the cold December wind and circled the crime scene again. The snow crunched under her boots and her breath came out in wisps of steam as she neared the newest victim. She was waiting for James to meet her before talking to the pathologist. While she waited, she tried to get a feel for the crime scene to be better able to determine what happened. They were in a park, about ten minutes away from her house, only a few meters away from a marked path that was often used by joggers. A single bush hid the victim from passersby. Knowing that Amy and Kyle spent a lot of time in this park made Maya nervous. She often jogged this same route and her daughter played sports in the field nearby. She shook off the feeling of uneasiness and got back to work. Not seeing anything else of significance, Maya again crouched down next to the corpse.

"So you think this is number two?" James asked, coming out of nowhere and crouching down next to her. Maya nodded absently as she considered the victim.

"Twenty-three year old female apparently jogging in the park when she was attacked. The body was found by a couple who were out walking their dog. The dog took off into the bush and the man went after it and found the body about forty-five minutes ago." Maya explained and James nodded. The victim was dressed in black leggings and a brightly colored jacket that was typical of the area joggers. Her jacket and long-sleeved t-shirt were torn across most of the front, exposing her chest and she was wearing only one black glove. Her black headband had come off and was lying next to the girl's head.

"What makes you think it's the same guy that killed Gabriella Fabiolo?" James asked and Maya scooted over a little closer to the body where she carefully lifted the dead girl's torn jacket.

"First of all, she's the right type. She's young and obviously athletic, judging by the clothes she's wearing and the proximity to the jogger's trail. She also has a similar pattern of bruises, from what we can see." Maya told him, pointing out the bruises on the girl's chest, neck and face. Her nose appeared to be broken and there was blood covering most of her face that had obviously been the result of that fracture.

"But Gabriella was murdered in her home." James reminded her, but Maya was already convinced that it was the same guy.

"Maybe he thought it would be less noticeable if it was done outside." she suggested and James considered the idea carefully.

"You might be right, but I say we wait for the autopsy report before we decide that we're dealing with a serial killer." James suggested and Maya agreed, standing up straight and dusting herself off.

"I'll wait for the results, but I'm already convinced. It's got to be the same perp." Maya said as they walked away from the scene. James remained silent, knowing that it was futile to argue with his stubborn partner. He had worked with her long enough to know that once she made up her mind about something, nothing short of hardcore evidence to the contrary was going to change it. He also knew that she was usually right.

"So how's Amy? Has that kid bothered her again at school or is he still afraid of her?" James asked with a smirk on his face.

"I wouldn't know, she still isn't talking to me. I think she expects me to let her go to karate, but I'm not going to cave." Maya said and James turned serious again.

"That's not right. I've never met a girl who confides in her mother as much as Amy confides in you. It's been a week already. You guys have got to patch this up." James told his partner and she looked up at him with tired eyes.

"Don't you think I've tried? It's killing me that she won't talk to me. There's this awful tension whenever we're at home together and it's driving me crazy. But she needs to learn that this is serious. If she hits him again and gets expelled from school it'll totally ruin her record and hurt her chances of getting into university and that's if his parents don't sue us." Maya explained, venting her frustration.

"Amy's a smart girl Maya. I'm sure she gets it." James replied and Maya reached for the handle on the car door.

"I sure hope so." she said as she got into the car, signaling the end of the conversation.

છે

By Thursday Amy had had enough. Kyle had learned a new *kata* and was raving about the fun games they had played during warm-ups. Amy desperately wanted to go back to karate class. Kyle had also revealed that a special guest instructor was coming to Friday's class and he claimed that it was too great an opportunity for Amy to miss. So Amy spent all day at school coming up with a new way to approach her mother to hopefully convince her to let Amy go back to karate a day early. Amy hurried home from school only to find a hastily scrawled note on the kitchen table telling her that Maya would be working late again. Letting out a frustrated sigh, Amy did her homework and watched television until she could no longer stay awake. Realizing that she wouldn't get to speak to her mother until the morning, Amy went to bed.

Unfortunately, Maya left for work the next morning before Amy got up so Amy trudged towards Kyle's house looking more than a little unhappy.

"So I guess she said no." Kyle said when he saw the look on his friend's face.

"I couldn't even ask her, she got home after I went to bed and left before I got up and you know how she gets if I call her cell when it's not an emergency." Amy whined and Kyle nodded sadly. They walked a few steps before he reached over and stopped her.

"Why don't we stop by her office after school? If we hurry, we can take the bus downtown and still make it to karate on time. I'll even help you, we can beg her together." Kyle suggested and Amy turned the idea over in her mind. Her mother couldn't possibly refuse her in front of Kyle and all her colleagues. Besides, it wasn't like she was being unreasonable, this was supposed to be the last day of her punishment anyways, she was just asking to be excused a few hours early.

"I think that just might work. Let me get my karate stuff." Amy said as she turned around and ran back to the apartment. She smiled as she thought of the look her mother would have on her face when she realized that she was cornered. Amy couldn't wait to try it.

73

Chapter 5

"My legs were shaking so bad, I thought for sure I was going to fall!" Kyle was saying as they exited the elevator on the fifth floor of the building. Amy had spent a lot of time in the tall brown brick building throughout the years and she knew her way around well. Ever since her mother had become a detective and had moved up to the fifth floor, Amy had been coming more and more. She led Kyle confidently down the hallway, but stopped just outside the door to her mother's department. Maya and her co-workers were all housed in the same room with their desks scattered around the room in pairs. Maya's desk was in the far left corner of the room facing her partner's desk. Amy peeked around the corner into the room to see if her mother was there. She had spent the day planning out her approach and wanted to get it just right. Amy knew her mother well so she knew that if she didn't lay out the facts just right, Amy would never get to go to karate. Spotting her mother standing near her desk, Amy started to walk into the room, but stopped short when she took in the scene. Maya was standing next to a tall good-looking man that Amy had never seen before. That in itself wasn't odd. But the fact that Maya was holding his hand and getting way too close definitely was.

Amy tried to get out of the room and backed right into Kyle who started to protest.

"Shhh!" Amy shushed him, putting her hand over his mouth and dragging him around the corner. Kyle tried to talk around her hand, but she held it there firmly and silenced him with a glare. Satisfied, Amy turned back to the scene in the room.

"It's nice to finally meet you, Harry." James was saying as he shook the man's hand. Harry was several inches taller than James and looked very pressed and proper compared to the detective who generally dressed more for comfort than for style.

"Likewise. Maya has told me so much about you." Harry said with a distinct British accent. Amy's eyes narrowed as she watched her mother's hand brush his arm in a very flirtatious way.

"So where are you two headed tonight?" James asked politely. Harry smiled down at Maya and Amy could see his brilliant white teeth from where she stood. The shine was so intense it would probably blind anyone who got too close. The man looked like a James Bond wannabe and Amy disliked him instantly.

"Maya has agreed to let me take her somewhere new tonight." he said and Amy got the impression that her mother had been on many dates with this man before tonight. James' hand flew to his chest as he feigned a heart attack.

"Somewhere new? You mean you're actually going to eat somewhere other than Mac's, Piero's and that Chinese place?" James asked his partner, looking surprised and amused. Maya swatted him playfully and he burst out laughing.

"Yes we are. I'm not afraid to try something new, I'm just partial to the restaurants that I already know are good." Maya said and Amy's mouth dropped open. Not only did her mother never eat anywhere but her three favorite restaurants, but she also never talked like that.

"I'm *partial* to the restaurants that I already know are good?" Amy repeated in a forced whisper. Kyle chuckled behind her, hiding his mouth behind his hand. Amy was speechless. Her mother never dated. Not only did Maya not date, but she never went crazy over a guy. She hung out with guys all the time. Most of her friends were guys. And though Maya was definitely beautiful and sexy and wasn't afraid to dress that way, she would probably beat up any of said guys who tried to put a move on her. It had always been that way… until now.

"Let's go." Amy said, grabbing Kyle's arm and dragging him towards the elevator. He hopped along next to her, grimacing and whimpering at the tight hold she had on him. He scowled at her when she finally let him go.

"What the hell was that for? What's going on?" he demanded once they were safely in the elevator.

"My mom has a boyfriend." Amy said slowly, still not quite believing what she had just witnessed.

"So, what's the big deal?" Kyle asked as he pushed his glasses higher up on his nose.

"My mom doesn't date! And it sounds like this isn't the first date either! She's been going out for God knows how long with this British bozo who looks like James Bond in a Colgate commercial and she never even told me! How is that not a big deal!" Amy shouted, gesturing wildly with her hands. Kyle took a step back and held up his hands in defeat.

"Okay, I'm sorry. This is not a good thing. I get it now." he said, trying to pacify her. The elevator door opened and Amy stormed out while Kyle hurried to keep up with her.

"Wait up Amy! We didn't even ask your mom if you could come to karate." Kyle said as he fell into step beside his friend.

"We don't need to. We'd better hurry up or we'll be late for class." Amy said, her face was expressionless, but Kyle could tell from the way she clenched her jaw that Amy was upset. He also knew from previous experience that it was best not to argue with her when she was angry. So they hurried out of the building and hopped on the next bus.

❧

They made it to karate just in time to bow in. There were four extra black belts present and one small Japanese man wearing a ratty looking red belt. Kyle gulped as he waited for the man to say something. This was the *Shihan* they had heard so much about. He was a master teacher and had more knowledge of karate than everyone in the club combined. The first thing they did was split up into groups according to rank.

"Okay, white, yellow and orange belts, you are with *Shihan*. He's going to teach you *Gekisai Ichi*." *Sensei* said naming a new *kata*. Kyle looked over at Amy excitedly as they hurried over to the other side of the gym.

"That's an orange belt *kata*!" Kyle whispered excitedly and Amy gave him two thumbs up. The kata was fun, but a little more complicated than they had expected. By the time they were done, Kyle felt confused, exhausted and proud of himself because he had kept up with the others. The more he applied himself at karate, the more Kyle saw that he wasn't as uncoordinated as he thought he was. Amy usually picked up the moves faster than he did, but he was getting better and better.

"That's the best kata yet!" Kyle said as they guzzled water during the break.

"That's only the third kata you learned Kyle!" Amy said with a grin.

"Still, it's definitely the coolest one." Kyle persisted and Amy chuckled.

"If you say so." she said. They both hurried back out when Sensei called them back for the second half of class. This time, two of the black belts from a nearby club gave an hour long lesson in self-defense. They learned how to escape head locks and holds and how to avoid roundhouse punches. They even practiced what to do if someone was to grab their hair. It was enlightening and fun and they spent most of the time laughing.

"We're all going to meet for wings at the sports bar down the street. If anyone needs a ride there, just wait out front and I'm sure someone will be able to bring you." Sensei said and Kyle sighed wistfully as he went to the change room to shower and change. He wanted to go out with everyone but knew that Amy would never be allowed to go, especially since she was supposed to be grounded. Kyle said goodbye to the guys and headed out. He was surprised to see Amy waiting out front with the others.

"We should hurry or we're going to miss the bus." Kyle told Amy. She didn't move from where she perched on the arm of a stone bench near the front doors of the College.

"Why run for the bus when Dave here already offered us a ride?" Amy said and Kyle stopped and looked back to where Amy was sitting next to Dave. He couldn't believe that she would actually dare to defy her mother twice in one day. Amy never lied to her mother. At least not until he asked her to.

"Because you're still grounded and your mom owns a gun." Kyle said, stepping closer to her and giving her a pointed look. She just waved off his protests and grinned wickedly.

"My mom is on a date, remember. She won't be home until late. Besides I wasn't supposed to come to karate either." Amy said, but Kyle wasn't convinced. He wanted to go out with the others, but he didn't want to push Maya too far. Maya and Amy were his only family and he didn't want to lose that. The others were looking at him, waiting to see what he was going to say. Not wanting to look like a loser, he swallowed his arguments and forced a smile.

"Cool, let's go." he said and Amy's smile lit up her face. She bounced to her feet and picked up her bag, before following Dave out to the parking lot.

∾

Sensei and *Shihan* had yet to arrive by the time the drinks got to their table. Dave pushed away his beer and turned to Kyle and Amy.

"No one drinks until *Shihan* does. Rank privileges, you know." Dave said and Amy quickly put her soft drink down.

"Good to know." she said, throwing a smile his way.

An hour later, they were just starting into the wings. The guys were already on their third pitcher of beer and Kyle wished he were old enough to drink. He stared glumly at his half empty glass of pop and reached for another wing.

"Hey, how do you like the wings?" Charles asked, coming to sit beside him.

"Awesome." Kyle answered after swallowing his mouthful.

"Yeah, they're not bad. Not quite hot enough, but we know better than to complain now." Charles said and Amy laughed.

"Why? Did you learn that the hard way?" Kyle asked and Charles laughed.

"Did we ever! It was probably four of five years ago when we first started to come here. We were feeling pretty macho and hassled the waiter about the wings. We told him that his hot wings were sissy wings and then we made the mistake of ordering more. When he brought the wings out, they were coated in neon orange sauce that was so bright we practically had to wear sunglasses." Charles said and Kyle and Amy burst out laughing.

"Oh my God! Were they edible?" Amy asked, watching him with a rapt expression on her face, totally engrossed in the story.

"We tried to eat them, but these wings were brutal. I swear my lips just about caught on fire as I was bringing the wing up to my mouth. My face was all red and tears were pouring down my face and I was sweating so much that I wanted to strip naked, but I forced myself to eat that wing. We finished all the wings because *we* didn't want to be the sissies. Let me tell you, we were begging for milk, vegetables, ice cream, anything to put out the inferno in our mouths." he answered. Most of the people at the table had tuned into his story and they all laughed as he finished.

"It's true, they were awful. They were so hot that you couldn't even taste the sauce anymore." Sensei corroborated and we laughed even more. Kyle was having such a good time that he didn't want to leave. Charles turned out to be an excellent story teller, especially once he had consumed a few more beers. They listened intently to all the stories about Sensei chasing off weird club members and tournament drama. When Amy finally looked at her watch, she gasped.

"What time is it?" Kyle asked with a frown.

"It's already past eleven o'clock. I've gotta go." Amy said, excusing herself and seeking out the waiter to pay her bill. Kyle hurried after her and then came back to get his coat. He was surprised when Dave offered to give them a ride home. They accepted gratefully and arrived home fifteen minutes later. Kyle watched from his front door as Amy hurriedly let herself into the apartment building. He prayed that Maya was still out with that guy and wouldn't notice that Amy had ducked out for the night.

He let himself in as quietly as possible and cringed when he saw the light on in the kitchen. He crept towards the stairs, dreading what he would see. He could hear his father yelling and knew that it wouldn't be good. As he passed the entrance to the kitchen, he hazarded a look inside and saw a man with a knife in his hand, threatening his father. His father was pinned with his back to the cupboards and the knife to his throat. Kyle could feel his heart pound and heard the blood rushing in his ears. He stood rooted in place, unsure of whether he should run or try to help his father. His father was pleading with the man, but he was slurring his words and he was obviously wasted.

"You know I wouldn't short change you on purpose! Come on man, it was an accident! It won't happen again." he was saying. Disgusted, Kyle ran up to his room, locking the door behind him. He brought his desk chair over and wedged it under the doorknob. Deciding that the frail chair wouldn't pose much of an obstacle to the drugged-up poster boy for the Hell's Angels that was downstairs, he pushed the chair out of the way and used all of his strength to move his dresser in front of the door. Hoping that it would be enough to keep him safe, Kyle curled up on his bed. All the self-defense he had learned today wouldn't stand a chance in hell against the man's knife or the gun that he probably had stashed in the glove compartment of his car. Not for the first time, Kyle wished that he was bigger and stronger and that he was good enough at karate to be able to fight off serious goons like the one that was hassling his father. He kept his clothes on and made sure that he had money in his wallet. He wanted to be prepared in case he had to make a quick escape. He sighed as he lay in bed, staring up at the ceiling. It was going to be another long night.

❧

Amy unlocked the door to the apartment and crept inside. When she saw that all the lights were on, she knew that she was busted. Not seeing her mother anywhere, she hurried towards the hallway, hoping to make it to her room before her mother spotted her. Maybe Maya had just gotten home and hadn't yet noticed that Amy was missing. With this in mind, Amy tore off her jacket and practically ran towards her bedroom.

"Don't even think about it." came a voice from the living room. Amy stopped and took a deep breath before turning to face her mother. Maya was sitting on the sofa with her arms crossed over her chest.

"Does the word 'grounded' mean anything to you?" she asked sarcastically and Amy flinched, but didn't answer.

"What is going on with you? This is the second time you stay out late without calling. I wasn't joking when I said that you were grounded. This isn't like you Amy." Maya said with an edge to her voice. Amy stared at the floor feeling contrite.

"Sorry." she muttered, but Maya wasn't appeased.

"Sorry isn't good enough. You lied to me Amy. I was worried sick about you. I had no idea where you were. I've been working night and day to solve the murders of two young girls. Do you have any idea how I felt when I couldn't find my own daughter?" Maya continued and Amy bristled.

"I never lied to you. I just didn't tell you that I was going to karate. I was going to ask you first but I haven't seen you in days." Amy stated, getting angry.

"Don't even try that one Amy. Omission is the same as lying." Maya said and Amy dropped her things on the floor and crossed her arms angrily.

"Then I guess you should stop lying to me." Amy said in a low voice. Maya's eyes narrowed and her frown deepened.

"Don't make this about me Amy. I never lied to you." she said, standing up and taking a step closer to her daughter. Amy took a step back and glared at her mother.

"I saw you with him today. I went to the station with Kyle to ask you if I could go to karate and I saw you with him. Why didn't you tell me you had a boyfriend?" Amy asked, trying to keep the hurt from entering her voice.

"I don't have to ask your permission to go on a date." Maya said, putting her hands on her hips. Amy's anger was fueled even more by her mother's defensive attitude.

"Who dates a guy named Harry?" Amy said sarcastically, suddenly wanting to hurt and embarrass her mother as much as she had been hurt.

"Who I date is none of your business." Maya said, practically spitting out the words. Maya had never spoken to her daughter this way. They were like best friends. They told each other everything and rarely argued. This tension was new for both of them and Amy felt that she could no longer handle it. She felt like she had just had a blowout with her best friend and all she wanted to do was go home and complain to her mother about it. Mothers were supposed to be there to support their children and make them feel better. Except her best friend was her mother and there was no one else to go to. Amy turned her back and fled to her room, before her mother could see her tough exterior crumble.

છ

Maya watched her daughter retreat and blew out a frustrated breath.

"Why am I the one that feels guilty?" she muttered to herself. She knew that she should still be angry at her daughter, but instead she felt guilty. She had been meaning to tell Amy about Harry, but had been putting it off, afraid of how her daughter would react. She had gone out to dinner with him this evening, but had come home early, hoping to spend some time with Amy. She had barely seen her daughter in weeks. Ever since that first girl died, she and her partner had been putting in crazy hours at work trying to catch her killer. Maya felt awful for leaving Amy alone all the time, especially since she was grounded and had to stay home. When Maya had come home and noticed Amy was gone, she had been furious. When Amy still hadn't come home by ten o'clock, Maya had seriously started to worry. She kept seeing those two dead girls and prayed that Amy wouldn't end up like them. Her relief was short lived when she heard Amy walk in. She had been so angry at her daughter, until she heard the hurt in her voice and saw it in her eyes. Now Maya just felt like the wicked witch of the west. She walked over to Amy's room and knocked on the closed door.

"Amy, can I come in?" she called through the door, letting her forehead touch the cool wood.

"No" came the muffled reply and Maya closed her eyes and sighed.

"We're not done talking about this Amy." Maya said. When there was no reply, Maya hesitated. There was no lock on her daughter's door, but she wasn't sure if she should just walk in or let her daughter cool off for a while. When she heard a muffled sob, the decision was made for her. Maya slowly opened the door and entered her daughter's room. In the lamplight, she could see Amy curled up on her bed with her back to the door. Maya walked over and sat on the edge of the bed.

"Amy…" she started, reaching over to lightly touch her daughter's shoulder.

"Go away!" Amy said, moving as far away as she could on the twin-sized bed.

"No, I won't. We are going to talk about this right now." Maya said firmly and Amy reluctantly sat up and wiped away her tears. She refused to look at her mother as she hugged her knees to her chest protectively.

"I'm sorry I didn't tell you about Harry. I wanted to wait and see if I was even going to like him before I told you." Maya explained patiently.

"How long have you been seeing him?" Amy asked, her voice wavering. Maya felt awful as she studied her daughter's tear-stained face.

"Almost a month. We only went out four or five times because I've been so busy with work." she revealed. Amy nodded and looked like she was about to say something when a fresh waved of tears over-came her. It nearly broke Maya's heart to see her daughter hurting so much. She pulled her daughter into her arms and rubbed her back as she cried.

℘

Amy hadn't cried on her mother like that since she was little. It felt so good to have her mother's arms around her. She hated the tension between them and wished that everything could go back to the way it used to be. Unfortunately, for that to happen, Amy would have to tell her mother everything and she couldn't do that to Kyle. She would just have to be strong and continue lying to her mother until Kyle saved up enough money to get away from his father. His life depended on her keeping her mouth shut. So she stifled a sob and pulled away from her mother. Maya watched her thoughtfully as she reached for a tissue and blew her nose.

"I'm sorry I went out without telling you. We had a bunch of special guests at karate today and I didn't want to miss it. I really did try to ask you first. Me and Kyle went to the station after school and we saw you with Harry. I heard you guys talking to James and I figured out that he was your boyfriend. I just got so mad because you didn't tell me about him that I went to karate without asking. Then everyone went out for wings after and I figured you would probably still be out on your date so I went with them. I didn't plan on staying out that long, I just lost track of time." Amy said and Maya listened carefully.

"You should have talked to me about it at the station instead of running away. If you would have asked me like you were planning to, I would have let you go to karate and I would have introduced you to Harry." Maya said calmly and Amy nodded.

"Honey, you know you can talk to me about anything, right?" Maya asked, holding Amy's gaze. Amy nodded, but didn't dare say anything. She wanted more than anything to tell her mother about Kyle's dad and let her deal with it, but she knew that she couldn't. Maya waited a moment, as if expecting Amy to say more. Amy ducked her head to avoid her mother's stare, but remained silent.

"Okay, well I know I should really punish you for what you did tonight, but I'm tired of being the bad guy. Let's just say that it was a huge misunderstanding between us and we'll leave it at that. Just promise me that you won't do it again. All I want is for you to tell me where you are so that I don't have to spend all my time worrying." Maya said and Amy sighed with relief.

"I promise." Amy said with a smile. Maya leaned over and gave her daughter another hug and a kiss before getting up and leaving. She was just about to close the bedroom door when Amy called out to her.

"Mom?" she called and Maya poked her head back in.

"What?" she asked. Amy warred with herself for a moment. She came close to blurting everything out to her mother but managed to stop herself.

"Thanks" she said lamely and Maya gave her a small smile.

"You're welcome. I love you, honey." Maya said, in a rare moment of tenderness.

"I love you too." Amy said and then lay back down in bed and pulled the covers up to her chin, praying for sleep to come quickly.

❧

Maya met James at the medical examiner's office to get the results of the two autopsies. They met the medical examiner and waited to see what she would have to say.

"Hey Karina, have you got something for us?" Maya asked as they approached the young woman. She was bent over the corpse of the young jogger they had picked up.

"Actually I do. I wanted to run something by you guys." she said and James got closer to the table.

"Shoot" he said and Karina peeled back the sheet that was covering the bottom half of the body.

"Something about the pattern of the bruising is bothering me. It's pretty much the same on both Gabriella Fabiolo and on Tiffany Rice. The first thing that jumped out at me was the broken knee. The point of impact was here, just above the knee and it was pushed outwards. It looks like someone gave it a very precise kick." Karina said and Maya frowned.

"Why is that so odd?" she asked and Karina stepped away from the body.

"If you were going to kick someone, where would you kick them?" Karina asked and Maya thought for a moment before answering.

"I guess I would kick them in the groin or in the stomach." Maya said and James nodded.

"Yeah, that would be my first instinct." he said, demonstrating with a slow kick.

"Exactly, so why is her knee broken at such a precise angle. It's highly unlikely that it was an accident. Also, there is bruising to the back of her head as if someone hit her with the side of their hand. That's not a normal way to hit someone either." Karina continued, lifting Tiffany's head to show the detectives what she was talking about.

"So this guy definitely knew what he was doing." Maya said thoughtfully and Karina nodded.

"Exactly. I think the fatal blow was actually the broken nose. He used an open-handed technique to hit her in the nose with an upward force. It propelled the bone into the brain matter." she explained and James flinched.

"Jeez. He definitely wasn't gentle." he said.

"Nope, she also has broken ribs and internal injuries consistent with strikes to the body as well as a broken elbow." Karina said. Maya frowned as she tried to put all the pieces together. Something about these injuries seemed vaguely familiar, but she couldn't quite figure out what that was.

"So do you have a theory about who could possibly inflict these kinds of injuries?" James asked Karina. The medical examiner was good at her job and often noticed things that went way beyond what was expected of her.

"I'm not sure, maybe someone in the army or a prison guard. Definitely someone who knows how to fight." she said with a shrug.

"Thanks a lot Karina. Let us know if you find anything else." James said and the detectives left the room with a lot on their minds.

༄

"We need to make one more stop." Maya told her partner, as they left the Sport Mart where Tiffany Rice used to work. She gave him the directions and then sat back in the passenger seat of the car and closed her eyes. She was tired. This investigation had them all working around the clock and she was starting to have trouble keeping up. When the car came to a stop, Maya reluctantly opened her eyes and got out. She followed her partner into the building and her heels tapped on the floor as they made their way to the end of the hall where they could see through the open door.

"Now are you going to tell me what we're doing here?" James asked as they walked in and took a seat off to the side.

"Research for our case. I think our attacker is an expert in martial arts, now we just need to see if I'm right." Maya said and waved to Amy who looked back at her with a confused look on her face. The karate class continued and Maya and James watched closely for any moves that could possible cause the injuries that their two victims had suffered.

"Look, open-handed technique to the face." Maya pointed out as the students practiced the move a few dozen times.

"And a kick to the knee. That's got to hurt." James noticed, ten minutes later, grimacing as if he had been hit.

"Amy and Kyle are pretty good. I'm impressed." James added. They waited until the class was over and then Amy came up to them.

"What are you guys doing here?" she asked as Maya and James stood up. The other students were looking over at them nervously. Maya and James definitely looked like cops and their presence tended to make other people nervous.

"We're doing a little research for a case we're working on. You guys are getting really good, by the way." Maya said as Kyle came over to join them. Both teens were sweating and their faces were red from the exertion.

"There's just one more thing that I'm not sure about. Did you guys learn how to break an elbow?" Maya asked curiously and Amy called out to one of the black belts that were passing by.

"Sensei Charles, my mom has a question for one of the cases she's working on. Do you think you could help her out?" Amy asked him and he came closer and extended his hand to Maya.

"Charles Nolin." he said with a smile.

"Hi, I'm detective Brendan and this is my partner detective Elliott. We're just wondering how someone who knows karate would go about breaking an elbow." Maya asked after introducing herself. Charles set down his duffel bag and moved back a few steps.

"Amy why don't you grab my wrist." He suggested and Amy complied. He put his other hand over top of Amy's and swung around so that she was behind him and then he pulled down on her arm until she tapped him on the shoulder and yelped in pain. He let her go instantly and looked over at the detectives.

"That's one way. Now punch me *Jodan*." he told Amy and she delivered a punch to the face. He blocked the punch and moved over to the side, keeping a hold on Amy's arm instead of just pushing it away. He then used an elbow strike to the arm to put pressure on the elbow until Amy signaled again to show that it hurt.

"There are many ways to do it, but we don't normally aim for elbows. Those moves are generally reserved for self-defense or more dirty fighting."

"Thank you very much. You've been very helpful." Maya said, before turning to her partner and throwing him an I-told-you-so look.

"Why don't you go get changed and we'll give you guys a ride home." James said to Kyle and Amy, ignoring his partner. They hurried off into the change rooms and he turned back to Maya.

"Okay so our guy probably knows karate." he allowed and Maya nodded, stuffing her hands deep into her coat pockets.

"And he's most likely good, because those moves are pretty precise. I doubt anyone at a lower level like Kyle or Amy could pull it off." Maya added and James nodded.

"So we might be looking for a black belt in karate, but what's the link between our victims and a karate sensei?" James asked. Maya just shook her head, deep in thought.

"I don't know, but we had better find out fast."

Chapter 6

"Okay so let's go over this again." James said as he and Maya sat at their desks facing each other. Their captain had come out of his office to listen to their brainstorming.

"So we have Gabriella Fabiolo. Her friends said that she jogged every morning." Maya started.

"And she was apparently an amazing swimmer; she was ranked sixth in all of Canada before she quit at the beginning of the year." James added and the captain nodded.

"We also found out that she did four years of Karate and got her blue belt before she quit two years ago." Maya said, shuffling some pages in front of her.

"Okay she obviously has an issue with sports since she quits as soon as they get too intense. What about Tiffany Rice?" the captain asked.

"Well she wasn't a swimmer, but she was a competitive runner. Her specialties were the endurance races. She also quit at the end of the spring semester. She obviously still liked to run, considering the fact that we found her just off the jogger's path in the park. Her friends confirmed that she ran whenever she wasn't working." Maya explained, leaning forward and placing her elbows on her desk.

"So the only commonality seems to be that they were amazing athletes who quit. Talk to their coaches and their families and find out why they quit and if anyone was upset enough about it to kill them." the captain ordered and both detectives grabbed their coat and hurried out of the office to comply with their request.

ళ

Two days before Christmas Eve, Maya was called to Amy's school. This time it wasn't for a parent-teacher conference or for a meeting with the principal. It was something worse.

Maya jumped out of the car and met the gurney just as it was being wheeled out of the school. The young girl was lying unconscious, her face a mess of blood and dirt.

"How is she?" Maya asked the paramedics that were wheeling her away.

"She's still unconscious and she lost a lot of blood, but her pulse seems strong. You'll have to wait until she sees a doctor to find out how bad her injuries are. Sorry, we have to go." the paramedic answered, loading the patient into the back of the ambulance and jumping in beside her. Maya watched with her hands on her hips as the ambulance sped away. James joined her a few minutes later and she filled him in.

"Well, she's alive, that's a switch." James commented and Maya frowned.

"Either it's not our guy, or he finally slipped up. Let's question some of the students." she suggested.

"You should probably ask Amy about her, too, she probably knew the girl." James said.

"Don't even go there. You know, this guy is really starting to make me nervous." Maya muttered as they approached the small crowd of people that had gathered. Since it was after school, the only people left at the school were teachers, some students in detention and the volleyball team practicing in the gym. They were all willing to talk and an hour later, the detectives had finished their interviews and were on their way to the hospital.

ও

"You're coming to my apartment for Christmas right?" Amy asked Kyle as they were walking home after karate class. He kicked at a chunk of snow on the sidewalk and buried his hands deeper in his coat pockets.

"I don't know Amy. Maybe that's not such a great idea." Kyle said, not daring to look up at her. A sudden stab of pain in his arm forced him to look up however. He cried out and rubbed the sore spot while turning to glare at his best friend who had just slugged him and was now glaring at him.

"What was that for?" he asked angrily and Amy stopped walking and put her hands on her hips. He couldn't help noticing that she looked exactly like her mother when she did that.

"That was for you being an idiot. What do you think my mom is going to say if you don't come over for Christmas? You spend Christmas with us every year. Don't you think she'll get a little suspicious if you suddenly decide not to show up?" Amy asked and Kyle grimaced. She had a point.

"I'll think about it." he said and they started walking again. Seeing that there were no cars in the driveway at Kyle's house, they headed towards the door.

"I think it's safe to come in. We'll just finish that project and then we won't have any homework for the rest of Christmas vacation." Kyle said as he turned the doorknob. In one of Ken Thompson's extremely rare moments of actually being nice to his son, he had bought him an amazing computer. Amy had recently decided that Mr. Thompson had probably stolen the computer or bought it off of someone else who had stolen it, but she didn't dare share her theory with Kyle. That computer was the one possession that he cherished and she didn't want to ruin that. She also appreciated the fact that he actually had a computer that worked and had the programs that they needed to complete their project. Her computer at home sucked and she kept hoping that her mother would just give in and buy them a new one. Then again, Maya had never been very good with computers so that probably wouldn't happen any time soon.

They walked into Kyle's house and crept past the kitchen. Amy didn't even dare to look into the kitchen for fear of what she might see. She looked straight ahead and followed Kyle as he started up the rickety staircase. She winced when the first step creaked under her weight, but forced herself to continue when all she wanted to do was run out the front door and go home. She was halfway up the stairs when she was suddenly yanked backwards by her hair. She screamed and reached up to grab the hand as she felt herself falling backwards. She tumbled down the stairs just to be yanked back up by the arm. Then she felt a blow to the face as she was knocked back down.

"Dad, stop! Amy didn't do anything!" Kyle yelled, stepping between Amy and his father. Mr. Thompson threw Kyle against the wall before he staggered back a few steps, breathing hard. Amy hazarded a look up at him and noticed that he was sweating and his eyes were glazed over. He had a wild look on his face and Amy bet he probably didn't recognize either of them. When he staggered back into the kitchen, Amy pulled herself to her feet and reached over for Kyle. They both hurried up the stairs to Kyle's room and locked the door behind them. They stayed there in the dark for a few minutes until Kyle finally flipped on the light and gasped.

"Amy! Your nose is bleeding!" he exclaimed and grabbed some Kleenex for her from a box on his dresser. Amy took them gratefully and dabbed at the blood that was slowly leaking from her aching nose.

"I'm so sorry Amy." Kyle said with an anguished look on his face. Amy took a deep breath to calm herself and then forced a smile on her face.

"It's okay. It's not your fault. He's so high right now I doubt he even knows where he is." Amy said, her voice sounding funny as she held the tissues to her nose.

"He didn't like break your nose or anything did he?" Kyle asked, haltingly. He tried to get a good look at Amy's face around the Kleenex.

"I don't think it's broken. Relax Kyle, it's all good." Amy said, tossing the Kleenex into the garbage can and gingerly touching her cheekbone and around her eye.

"Your eye is already all red. You're gonna have an awesome shiner tomorrow!" Kyle said with a grin, trying to lighten up the moment.

"At least it's a good excuse not to get my picture taken at Christmas." Amy answered with a smile. She hated having her picture taken.

"You see Kyle, there is a bright side to everything."

❧

Maya waited rather impatiently in the hallway outside their latest victim's hospital room. They had since learned that her name was Vanessa Mailloux and that she was only seventeen years old. She was the best high jumper in the city and had just recently given up the sport, but only temporarily, in order to concentrate on her studies in her senior year.

"Stop pacing, you're making me dizzy." James complained as he leaned back against the wall with his arms crossed. Just then the doctor came out of the room and Maya pounced on him.

"How is she doing doctor?" she asked.

"She's conscious and her vitals are stable. She suffered a broken elbow and a broken nose, but other than that she's fine. There shouldn't be any lasting damage." The doctor answered, flipping the chart closed.

"Can we speak to her?" James asked, moving forward to stand next to his partner.

"Be my guest, her mother is in there with her now." The doctor answered and the detectives thanked him before entering the room. The girl looked so young that Maya had to take a deep breath to steady herself before speaking.

"Hi Vanessa. I'm Maya and this is my partner James, we're the detectives working your case. Do you think you're up to answering a few questions for us?" she asked gently, moving over to stand near the head of the bed. The girl cowered in the big hospital bed looking very upset. She nodded almost imperceptibly and Maya cocked her head and gave the girl a small smile.

"Can you tell us what happened?" she asked slowly. Vanessa gulped and took a moment before answering.

"I was outside by the track. I wanted to practice my triple jump in the fresh snow. Then someone grabbed my arm and twisted it and broke my elbow. He moved so fast that he was behind me before I could do anything. Then he twisted me around and hit me in the face and I blacked out. That's all I remember." she said, her voice wavering. The pain was evident on her face as was the fear.

"What did he look like?" Maya asked and looked over at James to see him taking notes on his small notepad.

"I-I didn't really see him. It all happened so fast." Vanessa said.

"That's alright. Anything you can remember will be helpful." Maya assured her.

"Was he tall?" she asked, trying to get some kind of picture of this murderer.

"He was taller than me I think and he was very strong. Kind of like him, I guess." Vanessa ventured, pointing at James.

"Can you remember what color his hair was?" Maya asked, prodding gently.

"I'm not sure… I think it was dark." Vanessa said and tears started to roll down her cheeks as she got more and more frustrated.

"Please detectives, I think she's had enough." the girl's mother said, looking almost as distraught as her daughter.

"Of course. You did an excellent job Vanessa, thank you very much. I hope you feel better soon." Maya said before walking out of the room with her partner.

❧

Maya was still thinking about Vanessa when she got home that night. She draped her coat over one of the chairs in the kitchen and went into the living room where Amy was watching TV with Kyle in the dark.

"Hey guys. Why is it so dark in here?" she asked, plopping down wearily on the couch next to her daughter and reaching over to turn on a lamp. It took a few minutes before she noticed her daughter's face.

"What happened?" she asked, surprised. Amy glanced away and shared a look with Kyle.

"Sensei was using me for a demonstration at karate and he hit me by accident. It was my fault, I should've backed up." Amy said. Maya looked from her daughter to her friend, noticing the bright red flush that was creeping up Kyle's neck and face. Amy definitely wasn't telling her the whole story. Maya held Amy's chin with one hand and gently prodded the reddened area with the other, wanting to make sure that nothing was broken. Amy winced, but didn't pull away. Satisfied, Maya lay her head back against the couch cushions, too tired to make Amy tell her the truth. She couldn't, however, shake the uneasy feeling that the familiar placement of the bruise brought on. She glanced over at Amy again and her thoughts drifted back to Vanessa Mailloux, whose face was much more damaged than Amy's. But still...

಄

Christmas morning, Amy and Maya joked around as they made breakfast. They made pancakes and sausages and bacon and made a lot so that a certain someone could eat until he was full.

"Where's Kyle? He's usually here by now." Maya asked as she flipped a pancake. She had dressed for the occasion in a brown skirt and a red sweater. Her hair was pulled back in a French twist and she had carefully applied a minimal amount of makeup. Following her mother's lead, Amy had dressed in beige pants and multicolor striped V-neck sweater. She had opted to leave her hair down however in the hopes of hiding her black eye. Amy smiled at her mother and reached for the phone to call Kyle. He answered on the second ring, sounding sleepy.

"Kyle Thompson, what are you doing sleeping in on Christmas morning? If you don't get here soon I'm going to eat all your bacon." Amy threatened.

"I don't think I'm gonna come Amy.." Kyle started, but Amy cut him off.

"You can't bail out on Christmas!" she exclaimed, losing her smile. Maya put down her spatula and took the phone from her daughter.

"If you're not over here in ten minutes, I'm going over there to get you." Maya said into the phone and Amy's eyes widened, knowing just how much of a threat that was for her friend.

"Good choice." Maya said after a pause and then hung up the phone.

"He'll be right over." she said with a self-satisfied smile. Amy sighed in relief, knowing that the situation could have ended differently. She placed the plate of bacon and sausages on the table and adjusted the place settings.

"Are you sure there's nothing you want to add to your story?" Maya asked out of nowhere, resting a hip against the counter and facing her daughter. Amy felt t beat faster, but she tried to remain calm.

"What do you mean?" she asked, pretending to be confused.

"Your eye Amy. That doesn't look like an accident to me." Maya said, cocking her head to one side.

"Well it was." Amy said defensively, turning her back to her mother and rearranging the plates for the third time.

"If you're in trouble I can help you, but I can't do anything until you tell me what's going on." Maya pressed, taking a step forward and rubbing her daughter's arm. Amy flinched and pulled away as Maya touched her bruises. Maya grabbed Amy's wrist and pushed up her sleeve to see the finger marks that were again bruised into her daughter's flesh. She sighed as she dropped Amy's arm.

"Let me guess. It was karate right?" Maya said sarcastically. Amy was saved from having to answer when Kyle walked in.

"We'll talk about this later." Maya muttered, before pasting on a smile and turning to give Kyle a hug.

"Merry Christmas" she said cheerfully, holding him tightly for a moment. Amy thought she saw tears in his eyes and a wistful look on his face as he hugged her mother, but she couldn't be sure. Kyle had dressed up as well, in a pair of black corduroy pants and a button down shirt although he apparently hadn't managed to tame his hair since it was still standing on end.

"You look nice, Maya." Kyle said, almost shyly, his cheeks reddening slightly.

"Thanks Kyle." Maya said with a smile, turning back to the stove to flip the last of the pancakes.

"I hope you're hungry because we made tons of food." Amy broke in moving to sit down at the table. Kyle joined her eagerly and his eyes widened at the sight of the steaming plates heaped high with food in front of him.

"Dig in, guys." Maya said while she finished cooking. Both teens eagerly attacked the food. Maya noticed how Kyle seemed to inhale his breakfast and she wondered again if he really was neglected or if his father was just distant.

After breakfast, they all gathered in the living room around the tiny tree to open their gifts. Amy put on some Christmas music while Maya curled up on the couch with her camera.

"Come on mom, you don't really want pictures of me with a black eye do you?" Amy protested, but her mother held fast to the camera.

"It's Christmas. It's the one time of year that I'm guaranteed to get pictures of you so quit complaining." Maya said and took aim with the camera.

"Fine." Amy grumbled good-naturedly, grabbing Kyle around the neck and grinning. Maya snapped the picture and then pointed to the presents waiting under the tree.

"Go ahead." she said and Amy rubbed her hands together excitedly before reaching for the nearest gift.

"It's for you Kyle, from my mom." Amy said as she handed him the rather large package. He smiled and gratefully took the gift. He tore off the wrapping paper while the other two looked on. He pulled open the department store box and was elated to find a brand new winter coat in the box. He pulled it out and held it against him as he looked back and forth between Amy and her mother.

"Thank you so much! I-it's awesome." he stammered. He felt awkward accepting such an expensive gift from someone else's mother, but he was also touched that she had taken the time to buy him something that he really needed. He unzipped the jacket and tried it on, feeling right away how warm it was. It fit perfectly and had a working zipper, he couldn't ask for more.

"That looks good Kyle." Amy said with a knowing smile. Kyle posed for the camera and Maya snapped a picture. Then Amy reached for another gift and Kyle slowly took off the jacket and folded it back into the box. He considered himself very lucky to have Amy and Maya in his life. If it wasn't for them, Christmas would have been a very dreary holiday. Now it was turning out to be the best day ever. They always made him feel like part of their family, which was all he ever really wanted. He wanted so much to be part of a real family, with someone who loved him as much as Maya loved her daughter. She might not say it often and she might spend most of her time acting like a cool friend rather than a mother, but Kyle could tell that she really loved Amy and he was sure that Amy knew it. They all groaned when Maya's phone rang.

"I know, I know." Maya said, holding her hands up. She reached for the phone and turned it off without answering it.

"Better?" she asked, tossing the phone onto the chair in the far corner of the room.

"Much." Amy said, breaking into a huge grin.

Amy got a new MP3 player and some clothes from her mother. She gave Maya a trendy necklace and a brown and beige pin striped blouse as well as a movie, *Bon cop Bad cop* that she promised was an awesome movie.

"A cop movie? Why am I not surprised?" Maya said with a laugh.

"It's really good, I swear!" Amy exclaimed and Maya leaned forward to give Amy a hug.

"Thank you sweetheart." she said and Amy grinned. Kyle reached for a small box that he handed to Maya. She looked surprised, but smiled at him and slowly tore off the paper. Opening the box, she found a dainty silver bracelet nestled inside.

"It's beautiful Kyle!" she exclaimed and Kyle blushed again.

"It's not much, but I thought it would look good on you." he said and Maya motioned for him to come closer.

"Come over here and fasten it for me." she said, holding the bracelet on her wrist. Kyle's clumsy fingers fumbled with the clasp, but he eventually got it on. Maya gave him a kiss on the cheek and held out her arm for Amy to inspect. Amy nodded her approval and then handed Kyle another fairly large package from under the tree. He had just started unwrapping it when there was a knock at the door.

"I'll get it. You guys continue." Maya said, getting to her feet and gingerly picking a trail trough the paper and boxes that littered the floor. The person at the door knocked again impatiently and Maya rolled her eyes before opening the door. James stood on the other side, dressed in his usual suit and tie and long trench coat. He had one arm resting on the doorframe and the other was lifted, ready to knock again.

"Come in. You're late, we're almost done unwrapping all the presents." Maya said and started to walk back into the apartment. James caught her arm before she could go back into the living room. He quickly shut the door and then gave his partner a meaningful glance. She groaned and pushed a stray hair behind her ear.

"Not today! Don't tell me there was another one today!" Maya said, sounding tired and disappointed.

"Another high school kid as she was leaving gymnastics practice." James confirmed.

"It's Christmas for God's sake! Why can't the bad guys take a break for one day?" she asked with a frustrated sigh.

"Beats me. I tried calling you but you didn't answer." he said and Maya looked guilty for a moment.

"I turned off my phone. I figure my daughter deserves to at least have me home for Christmas." Maya stated and James nodded but didn't say anything.

"I even wore a damn skirt because I was trying to be festive!" Maya whined whirling around and heading back into the living room where Kyle was raving about the karate pattern sweatshirt Amy had given him along with a pair of *kumite* mitts used for fighting. Both kids were laughing as Maya sat back down on the couch. James perched next to her on the arm of the sofa.

"Look mom. We bought each other the same thing!" Amy exclaimed between fits of laughter, showing her mother the identical pair of *kumite* mitts that she was now wearing.

"Hey James, Merry Christmas." Kyle said as he recovered first. He pushed his glasses higher on his nose, before looking back over at Amy. She looked over at him at the same time and they both burst out laughing again. Maya thought he had never looked happier. His face was aglow and his smile actually reached his eyes for once. His rosy cheeks made him look healthier than she had seen him look in a while and he seemed to have totally relaxed. Aside from Amy's badly bruised eye and cheek, she also looked revitalized. Maya hated to have to be the one to ruin the happy moment.

"Well it looks like you guys got so many presents that you don't need mine." James said jokingly as he reached into his coat pocket and pulled out what looked like four tickets. Amy jumped to her feet and bounded towards him, full of energy.

"What is it?" she asked excitedly grabbing the tickets and holding them closer so that she could read them. She shrieked and threw her arms around James, nearly knocking him over in the process. He held her lightly while he chuckled over her reaction, looking very pleased with himself. Amy hurried over to Kyle to show him the tickets and Kyle pumped his fist in the air, looking even more excited.

"The Nickelback concert! You rock James!" he exclaimed and James nodded knowingly.

"I know." he said with a smug grin on his face. Maya looked amused as she glanced up at her partner.

"I thought we could all go together. It'll be fun." he told her and she nodded her agreement.

"I guess you are pretty cool." she said in a mocking voice and he reached over to tousle her perfectly coiffed hair. She shrieked and reached up to grab his hand. Super fast, she twisted his arm around so that she had him bent in half with his arm pinned behind his back. Amy and Kyle howled with laughter as she held him there for a moment.

"Don't ever touch my hair." she ordered and Amy stepped forward and to mess up James' hair as much as she could before Maya let him go. He pretended to look insulted as he raked his short hair back into place. Kyle gave Maya a high five and they touched fists like they normally did. James finally gave in and laughed along with them.

"Why don't you guys start cleaning up while I talk to James for a minute." Maya suggested as she waded through the sea of paper in an effort to make her way to the kitchen. James followed her and leaned against the counter.

"Okay so tell me about the new victim." she said.

"Amanda McCullough is fifteen and she is a relatively good gymnast. She was just leaving the gym when she was assaulted. She's still alive, but just barely. She was still unconscious when she arrived at the hospital." James explained, reading from his notepad.

"It doesn't make sense. He's lowering his standards. The first two victims were national level athletes who quit while they were at their peak and those attacks were weeks apart. It's like he took the time to research them and that's why there was a bigger gap between their murders. Everything was so well planned out. These last two girls are younger and they haven't reached their peak yet in their sports. Their attacks were only two days apart, so he probably didn't have time to research them." Maya said, trying hard to figure out how the attacks all fit together.

"Maybe he's feeling the need to attack these girls a lot stronger now. The high school girls were crimes of opportunity. They were obviously athletic, but he didn't take the time to make sure that really fit his profile. Now he's just attacking for the pleasure of attacking and he's getting careless, that's why these girls aren't dead." James added. Maya nodded her understanding and then looked back at the two kids in the living room. She sighed and started to leave the room.

"Just give me a few minutes to change and we'll go to the hospital." Maya said over her shoulder.

"Why don't you stay here for now?" James suggested and Maya stopped short. She turned to look at him with a frown on her face.

"What are you talking about?" she asked confused.

"Andrighetti and Michaels are already at the crime scene and I can interview Amanda alone. She might still be unconscious anyways. You're right. You should be here with those kids. They deserve to have a good Christmas. Just look at how happy they are." James said, motioning towards the living room. Maya turned to look and stifled a smile when she saw Amy pelting Kyle with wadded up paper and ribbons. He was laughing as he protested half heartedly, his arms held protectively in front of his face.

"Are you sure?" Maya asked, not wanting to shirk her duties.

"I'll call you if I need you." James promised and Maya felt extremely relieved.

"Did I ever mention that you are the greatest partner ever?" Maya said enthusiastically as she looped her arm loosely around his neck and gave him a quick squeeze.

"Now that you mention it…" James started and Maya laughed and pointed a warning finger at him.

"Don't push your luck." she warned as she opened the door for him.

"Bye guys!" he called out to Amy and Kyle.

"Bye James, thanks a lot for the tickets!" Amy called back, stopping to wave at him.

"Yeah thanks! Merry Christmas!" Kyle echoed happily and James waved back.

"Yeah thanks James." Maya said quietly, leaning against the open door.

"Don't worry about it." James said, straightening his jacket and stepping out into the hallway. Maya was about to shut the door when he stopped her.

"Just do me a favor and turn your phone back on."

Chapter 7

"This isn't the end of the world Amy. Stop acting like I'm forcing you to commit murder or something." Maya whispered forcefully as she led her daughter across the restaurant to a table at the back where a man was waiting for them.

"Whatever. I just don't see why you can't date someone who is more like James." Amy grumbled and then pasted on a fake smile when she felt her mother tighten her grip on Amy's shoulder. Harry slid gracefully out of his seat and stood to meet them.

"Harry, I'd like you to meet my daughter Amy." Maya introduced them and Harry gave Amy a dazzling smile as he shook her hand warmly.

"It's so nice to finally meet you." he said in his thick British accent. Amy had to force herself not to roll her eyes as he leaned forward and gave Maya a peck on the cheek. Then he held out Maya's chair for her and Amy made sure to sit down quickly before he could do the same for her. She already felt uncomfortable in the fancy restaurant and didn't want to draw attention to herself. Maya had made Amy dress up and now she tugged at the hem of her skirt that suddenly felt way too short. Maya on the other hand looked like she belonged with her hair carefully pinned back and her makeup accentuating her dark eyes. She was wearing a simple black dress that ended just above her knees and made her look sexy, yet classy. Amy frowned wishing she were at Piero's with James instead where everyone dressed in jeans. They always got free breadsticks because the owners knew them so well. Amy glanced at her water glass and was surprised to see that it was fizzy. She bet they didn't even give free water in this place.

"So Amy, your mother tells me that you enjoy doing karate." Harry said and Amy nodded. Maya threw her a pointed look and Amy sighed.

"Yeah, karate's cool." she said reluctantly.

"It's obviously a little rough, but I think it's good for girls to learn some self-defense." Maya added, trying make up for Amy's lack of communication.

"I agree. Have you been taking karate long?" Harry asked her next.

"Since September." Amy told him, slumping lower in her chair. The rest of the meal passed much like that. Harry and Maya eventually gave up in trying to get Amy to join in the conversation. Amy knew from the look on her mother's face that Maya definitely wasn't happy with her, but Amy didn't care. Even though Harry was a perfect gentleman all night, Amy found him extremely dull. He definitely wasn't the right guy for her mother.

Towards the end of dinner, Maya left for a moment to go use the restroom. Amy kept her eyes on her plate, trying to seem disinterested. Harry cleared his throat, obviously trying to get her attention, but Amy ignored him.

"You know Amy, I think very highly of your mother and I am beginning to care for her a great deal. It would be a real shame to have to put an end to a budding relationship because of a misunderstanding between us." Harry said and Amy looked up with a frown.

"I'm sure there is some way we can clear up this misunderstanding and start anew." he continued, pulling his wallet out of his pocket. He started counting out bills and Amy's jaw dropped.

"You're trying to bribe me!" she exclaimed, disliking him even more.

"Of course not, but I know your mother holds your opinion in high regard and I just want to make sure that you have the absolute right opinion of me." he said, not looking the slightest bit ruffled. Amy couldn't believe what this jerk was saying.

"In case you haven't noticed, my mother does what she wants." Amy told him crisply, her anger evident only in her eyes. Harry raised an eyebrow and leaned back comfortably in his chair, linking his fingers together over his chest.

"I'm sure she does. I am merely looking out for her, for what is in her best interests." Harry said smoothly and Amy had to press her lips together to keep from screaming at the man.

"My mom can take care of herself. She doesn't need you to interfere. Besides what the hell would you know about her best interests?" Amy said, shoving her chair back. Harry slowly shook his head, disapprovingly.

"That language." he said, but Amy couldn't care less.

"You know Amy, you might also want to consider what is best for your mother. She's at the point in her life where she wants to settle down with a family. She's tired of always taking care of everyone and everything. She longs for someone to take care of her for once. She wants to forget about her troubles, her troubles at work, her financial troubles, trouble with her family. She worries a lot Amy, mostly about you. Don't you want her to have piece of mind? I can give her that. I can give her stability and love. She's happy when we're together. Don't you want that for her?" Harry said and Amy was so confused she didn't know what to think anymore. She wanted to ignore everything that he was saying, but the more she thought about it, the more she realized that he had a point. She knew that her mother was lonely. She had naively thought that they could be a pair forever, just Maya and Amy. She wondered now though if Harry might have a point. Maya did deserve to be happy. Amy had thought that she was already happy, but what if she wasn't? With a sigh Amy pulled her chair closer to the table and leaned her head on her hand. Before she could think of a reply to Harry's tirade, she felt her mother's hand on her back and she jerked up in surprise.

"Sorry I took so long. There was actually a line-up, would you believe it?" Maya said sliding back into her seat and placing her linen napkin back on her lap. She glanced uneasily at Amy before turning to Harry and giving him a bright smile.

"Not a problem. I was just looking at the desert menu and the chocolate mousse looks scrumptious. Are you interested?" Harry said and Maya licked her lips excitedly.

"It's times like these that I'm glad I'm not a girl who counts calories." Maya said and Harry laughed.

"As am I." he assured her and Maya turned to Amy.

"Do you want some desert?" she asked her daughter, her smile fading a little as she waited to see how her daughter was going to react. Amy's eyes flickered up to Harry's and she saw that he was practically challenging her with his steady gaze.

"Sure, I'll have whatever you're having…please." she added as an afterthought. Maya looked surprised and relieved at Amy's sudden change in behavior. Amy made an effort to be pleasant throughout the rest of the meal. She said little and didn't smile much, but she wasn't rude either. She sensed her mother relax and noticed that she was indeed enjoying herself. Apparently Maya didn't find Harry nearly as boring as Amy did.

༄

When they got home later that night, Maya slammed the front door shut and whirled around to face Amy. Amy half expected to see smoke coming out of her mother's ears. That's how angry she was.

"What the hell is your problem? I can't believe how rude you were! Why Amy? Why were you trying to sabotage a perfectly good date?" Maya yelled, throwing her arms up in the air. Rather than get angry, Amy sighed deeply, suddenly feeling exhausted.

"I don't know. I'm sorry mom." Amy said quietly. Maya seemed taken aback by Amy's answer, or lack thereof.

"Are you mad because I'm dating or do you just not like him?" Maya asked, toning her voice down slightly.

"I'm not mad. Besides who you date is none of my business remember?" Amy said with a shrug. Maya closed her eyes and brought a hand up to massage her forehead.

"I didn't mean that Amy. It's important to me that you like who I date." Maya said in a calmer voice.

"He's okay, really. He's nice." Amy said, even though it pained her to do so. Maya's eyes narrowed.

"Did he say something to you while I was gone?" she asked, sounding suspicious.

"No. I'm really tired. Can I go to bed now?" Amy asked, just wanting the conversation to end before she blurted out the truth about Harry and ruined the first good relationship her mother ever had.

"Go ahead." Maya said, looking thoroughly confused. Amy felt listless as she dragged herself to her bedroom and flopped down on her bed. In the past few months she had been forced to grow up very fast. Between Kyle's problem and her mother dating, Amy always seemed to be faced with tough decisions. She had to watch every word she said and everything she did and it was very tiring. What she wouldn't give to just be an innocent child again.

Kyle was so hungry he could barely stand himself. Gathering his courage, he stepped out of his bedroom and listened for sounds of trouble. Not hearing anything, he crept as silently as he could towards the kitchen. He winced every time a floorboard creaked and he was so nervous that perspiration had broken out over his upper lip. He turned into the kitchen and scanned the room quickly before hurrying towards the fridge and yanking the door open.

"Its empty." a voice behind him said. Kyle jumped and whirled around in surprise. It took him a moment to find his father sitting on the floor in the corner of the room, rocking back and forth.

"You have to get me more Kyle. I need it so bad." he said in a shaky voice. Kyle nodded vehemently and stayed in place, wondering what to do.

"Just tell me when and I'll go meet him." Kyle said agreeably, not wanting to anger his volatile father.

"NO!" Ken yelled suddenly and began to rock faster. He was practically pulling his long greasy hair out of his head and Kyle wondered for the first time if his father was going to die.

"He won't sell it to you anymore. He said you're gonna get him caught. There's a guy at your school. He's gonna meet you in the room beside the gym tonight at nine o'clock. Do this for me buddy. There's money in the freezer. Take it. There's an extra twenty I think, you can have it. Buy yourself something nice." Ken said sounding more and more shaky by the minute.

"Okay Dad." Kyle said, opening the freezer and taking out the money. He had long since stopped questioning his father's logic and just did as he was told. It was safer that way. Stuffing the money into the pocket of his faded jeans, Kyle took one last look into the empty fridge and left with a sigh. He was just putting his shoes on when the phone rang. He snatched it up quickly before it could irritate his father and punched the talk button.

"Hello?" he asked, sounding slightly breathless.

"Hey Kyle, I have to talk to you. Do you want to go for a walk?" Amy asked him, not wasting time with pleasantries.

"I can't Amy. I have to run an *errand*." Kyle stressed, hoping that she would get the message and leave him alone.

"That's cool, I'll go with you. I'll be outside your house in a few minutes." Amy said, obviously not getting the hint. She hung up before Kyle could explain it to her and he slammed the phone down in frustration. He grabbed his coat and hurried out the door before Amy could find an excuse to come in and saw his dad.

He waited less than a minute before he saw her walking towards him with her hands stuffed deep into the pockets of her coat and her breath coming out in puffs of steam in the cold night. Kyle zipped up his nice new jacket and reveled in its warmth. They started walking and Amy started talking. She told him all about the date the night before and Kyle's mouth dropped open in surprise.

"He tried to bribe you!" he exclaimed, much as she had done. Amy nodded grimly, but went on to explain hurriedly.

"What he said made a lot of sense though. I mean my mom is still young, she should have a nice man to live with who can take care of her." Amy said and Kyle chuckled.

"I so can't picture your mom ever letting anyone take care of her." Kyle said with a grin.

"You should have seen them together. The way she was looking at him." Amy shuddered, when she thought about it.

"She obviously likes him, though I have no idea why. I shouldn't be the one to screw it up for her." Amy explained and Kyle shook his head in disapproval.

"She should know that he's a jerk Amy. If she knew that he bribed you, she would dump him in a second. She might even punch him first. Hard." Kyle said, trying to keep a straight face even as he pictured the scene.

"That's why we're not going to tell her, right?" Amy demanded and Kyle shrugged.

"Whatever." he said as they turned the corner.

"Where are we going anyways?" Amy asked as they approached the school. Kyle hesitated before answering.

"We're going to buy drugs." he said nonchalantly. Now it was Amy's turn to look at him in disbelief.

"Are you serious?" she exclaimed and Kyle nodded.

"Yep, my dad needs them bad." he revealed and Amy tried to compose herself as she followed Kyle around to the back of the school.

"Okay, so we're going to buy drugs. It's all good." she muttered, more to herself than to him. She was obviously trying to convince herself that it was okay.

"Let's not tell my mom about this either, okay?" she said in a high pitched voice and Kyle laughed.

"Sure thing." he said, laughing more out of fear and nervousness than anything else. It was so dark that they practically had to feel their way around the building until they came to a door. Kyle yanked it open and silently thanked God for the fact that the lock was still broken on the gym door. Dim night lights bathed the gym in an eerie orange light.

"Why don't you wait in here while I... you know." Kyle suggested and Amy wasn't sure which was more frightening, the dark shadows in the corners of the gym or the image she had in her head of the drug dealer. The freaky drug dealer finally won and Amy nodded to Kyle. He made his way across the wooden floor and disappeared into the shadows. Amy turned around in a slow circle and shivered when she thought of what might be waiting for her in those shadowy corners.

"Suck it up karate girl!" she commanded herself and took up a fighting stance. She figured she might as well take advantage of the empty gym to practice her karate moves. After a few punches and kicks, Amy was feeling more confident. She forgot about the shadows and concentrated instead on getting the moves right on the new *kata* they were in the process of learning. She was totally caught off guard when someone grabbed her from behind and slapped a hand over her mouth before she could scream. She flailed her arms until the man caught one of them and twisted viciously. Moving on instinct, Amy twisted with him to save her elbow from being broken. Without thinking, she kicked as hard as she could and she heard the man draw in his breath sharply and release her as she connected with his groin. She tried to run, but he reached out a hand and grabbed her ankle. Amy went down hard, landing face-first on the hardwood. She rolled over onto her back as the man launched himself at her. He punched her in the face, but the movement was slowed down considerably by Amy's attempt at a block. His knees dug into her sides and his weight crushed her so that she could barely breathe. Panic threatened to overtake her, but Amy knew that if she let it, she would never make it out alive. When the man realized that he wouldn't get to her face easily, he wrapped his fingers around her throat. Black spots started to crowd Amy's vision as she struggled to breathe. She was about to give up when she heard what sounded like a stampede coming from the other side of the gym. The crashing sound went on for several seconds and was accompanied by the sound of balls bouncing and metal clanging. The man suddenly jumped up and ran away, scared off by the threat of discovery. Amy rolled over onto her side, gulping in air as Kyle came running up to her. He looked at her wide-eyed and helped her sit up.

"What happened Amy? Who was that?" he asked, awkwardly rubbing her back as she coughed and wheezed.

"I-I don't know! He just attacked me!" Amy told him, her voice rising hysterically before she starting to cry. Kyle awkwardly patted her back as her body shook with sobs.

"Are you okay? Did he hurt you?" Kyle asked eventually. Amy shook her head and wiped away the tears.

"I don't think anything's broken. Just a few more bruises I guess." Amy said, moving her arms and legs to assess the damage.

"We should get out of here." Kyle said and helped Amy to her feet. He slipped his arm around her waist and helped her limp out of the gym. By the time they reached the street, Amy was walking better although her ankle was throbbing and Kyle could see gashes on Amy's neck where the man had grabbed her.

"I guess you have to tell your mom." Kyle said sounding resigned.

"I can't tell my mom." Amy said forcefully.

"You were attacked! You have to tell her." Kyle insisted and Amy turned on him.

"What am I supposed to tell her? 'Hey mom, we were trespassing on school property and buying illegal drugs when I was attacked by some phantom bad guy.' She would totally freak out." Amy cried.

"Well you have to tell her something, you're bleeding." Kyle pointed out. Amy reached up and touched her neck. She was surprised to see blood on her fingertips when she looked at them.

"I'll think of something. Let's just go home this place is freaking me out."

Chapter 8

Amy stopped outside the door of her apartment and took a deep breath. She pulled her hood on and zipped up her jacket as high as it would go in an attempt to conceal her new wounds. Maya was already suspicious, Amy couldn't afford for her to figure out what was really going on. Amy walked into the apartment and shut the door behind her, taking her time in locking the deadbolt while she listened for signs of her mother. Maya obviously wasn't in the kitchen and it didn't sound like the TV was on, so Amy prayed that her mother was in her room reading or better yet, asleep. Hurrying down the hall, Amy escaped to the safety of her room and breathed a sigh of relief when she managed to shut the door behind her. She turned on the light and pulled off her jacket that she draped over her desk chair. Then she stepped closer to the mirror over her dresser and raised her chin so that she could examine the gashes left over from her attacker's unforgiving grip. She was trying to come up with ways to hide the marks when the door burst open.

"Have you seen my brown suede boots? I can't seem to find them an-" Maya was saying as she walked into the room. Amy whirled around surprised and her hand flew to her neck in an attempt to hide it from her mother's view. She knew she was too late when Maya's eyes widened and she stopped talking mid-sentence. Amy quickly turned her back to her mother and pulled open the top drawer of her desk. She searched blindly in the drawer for anything that could give her a clue as to what to do next.

"Amy" Maya said, but Amy continued to fumble in the drawer, for what she wasn't exactly sure.

"Amy look at me!" Maya commanded and Amy reluctantly turned around, but kept her head down. She was shaking from residual fear from the attack and from the tension of this confrontation. Amy swallowed hard to keep from crying. She averted her mother's gaze, knowing that with one look she could lose what little control she had over her emotions.

"I want you to tell me what happened and don't you dare say it was karate." Maya said slowly in a barely controlled voice.

"What do you want me to say, mom?" Amy yelled back, totally clueless as to what she was supposed to do to get herself out of this mess.

"We can't keep doing this Amy. Why can't you just tell me the truth?" Maya asked her voice breaking. Amy stared down at her hands that were scratched to hell from fighting off the attacker and used every ounce of willpower not to answer her mother. She was surprised when she heard her mother leave the room. She was even more surprised when Maya returned with a camera.

"Take off your clothes." Maya ordered and Amy retreated to the far side of the room.

"No way!" she cried, hugging her arms to herself. Maya came closer and Amy pressed herself against the wall.

"Take off your clothes or I'm calling the cops." Maya threatened and Amy's eyes flew to her mother's face. Maya's stony expression unnerved her and she reluctantly pulled off her shirt and her pants, feeling totally exposed in her bra and underwear even though it wasn't the first time her mother had seen her like that. When Maya saw the large bruises on Amy's torso and the scratches and finger marks on her hands and arms, she was forced to look away for a moment. Amy couldn't stop the few tears that escaped and ran down her cheeks. Maya lifted her daughter's chin and snapped a picture of the wounds on Amy's neck. Then she did the same for the rest of the bruises and scratch marks. When she was done, she left the room without a word and Amy shakily pulled on her pajamas and sat down on her bed. She wiped away her tears and pulled her knees up protectively. Maya came back a moment later with a bottle of peroxide and large gauze pad. Amy sat still while her mother dabbed peroxide on the gashes and taped the gauze over top of them. Even though she was obviously very upset with her daughter, Maya's touch was gentle and soothing and totally broke down Amy's defenses. Sobs escaped her and her body shook from all her pent up emotion. Maya pulled her close and held her tightly as she cried. Everything she had kept bottled up leaked out of her as she cried in her mother's arms. They rocked back and forth silently as Amy struggled to compose herself. When Amy finally calmed down, Maya pulled back and carefully wiped her own eyes. She waited a full minute before she spoke.

"Let's try this again. Just tell me who's hurting you and I'll get him. I won't ever let him hurt you again." Maya promised. Amy just shook her head and didn't answer.

"I know you're scared. I deal with abuse victims every day and they are all scared, but you don't have to take this. Let me help you baby!" Maya pleaded, but Amy shook her head again, choosing instead to look at the shag carpet that covered most of the floor in her room. With a frustrated cry Maya got up and marched out of the room. Amy waited until she was sure her mother was gone before getting up and closing the door. She climbed beneath the covers in her bed and reached for her ratty old bunny rabbit that she used to love. She was much too old for stuffed animals, but for just a minute Amy needed its comfort. She needed to feel the security she used to feel when she was a child, when her rabbit and her mother could solve all her problems.

✑

Maya paced back and forth in the tiny kitchen wondering what the hell she was supposed to do next. Something terrible was happening to her baby girl and she was powerless to stop it. Why couldn't Amy trust her? They had always told each other everything. Why would she hold back now, when it was most critical? Flipping open her cell phone she did what seemed most natural. She called James.

"Elliott." he answered on the first ring.

"It's me. Something's going on with Amy and I don't know what to do." Maya said, not wasting any time. She pressed the phone to her ear with one hand and held her stomach with the other. Just the thought of the abuse her daughter must have suffered made her nauseous.

"What do mean? What did she say?" James asked, sounding confused.

"She's covered in bruises again, she just cried on me for a good ten minutes and all she'll tell me is that it's from karate." Maya answered, trying to keep her voice from rising and making her sound hysterical.

"Has this been going on for a while? Did she say who was doing it?" James asked, sounding more concerned.

"I don't know. She won't talk to me." Maya said her voice breaking. She sat down at the table and put her head in her hands.

"I'll be right over." James said into the phone before hanging up. Maya let the phone fall onto the table and she allowed herself to cry. Her shoulders shook with sobs that she tried to stifle so that Amy wouldn't hear her. When there was a knock at the door ten minutes later, Maya had managed to pull herself together, but she was barely holding on by a thread. James took one look at her and pulled her into his arms for a quick hug. His kindness nearly made her break down again, but she forced herself to suck it up.

"Okay, so explain this to me again." James said, pulling out a chair and sitting down.

"Amy's been coming home with unexplained bruises for a while now. She keeps saying that it's from karate. That it's nothing. Then she got that black eye just before Christmas and there were finger marks bruised into her arm. She said her sensei hit her by accident during a drill. That's when I started to think something wasn't right. Then she came home tonight with scratches on her face and her hands and she has these awful gashes on her neck. Someone tried to choke her James. I'm sure of it. Some of the blood vessels in her eyes busted. This wasn't just some drill!" Maya explained, getting more and more worked up. She showed him the pictures on the camera and he whistled in appreciation.

"That bastard hit her hard. So who do you think it is?" James asked, frowning.

"I don't know. I think it might be the sensei. She at least admitted that he hit her once. Even if she said it was an accident." Maya rationalized and James nodded his agreement.

"I'll get Bill to check it out tomorrow. We'll check to see if anyone from the club has a record." James suggested and Maya seemed to sag with relief. At least something was finally being done.

"I was half hoping that I was just being overly sensitive because of the case." Maya admitted and James smiled sadly.

"Unfortunately, I think your mommy radar was working well this time. We definitely need to look into this, and soon. In the meantime, you need to try talking to Amy again. If anyone can get her to talk it's you. She idolizes you, you know." James said and Maya shook her head.

"For the five minutes I'm home you mean. This is my fault. I've been so absorbed in this case that I've barely even seen my daughter. God knows how long this has been going on." Maya said, getting more upset as she voiced her guilt.

"Don't do this to yourself Maya. You caught this before it's too late and that's all that matters." James said, reaching over to give her shoulder a squeeze. Maya gave him a small smile as she thanked God for the millionth time that she had him as a friend. Because as much as she liked to flaunt her independence, she really needed someone to lean on right now.

⁓

Amy was incredibly sore when she woke up the next morning. It was a struggle just to get out of bed and it took all her strength just to pull on sweatpants and a hooded sweatshirt. She thought about putting on a turtle neck sweater to hide her neck, but realized that her face was just as damaged and she nixed the idea. She limped into the kitchen, her ankle swollen and throbbing and slumped into one of the kitchen chairs. Maya looked up from where she sat across from Amy sipping her coffee and reading the morning paper. She didn't say anything as she turned the page and went back to her paper. Amy sighed and sank lower in her chair.

"Aren't you going to work today?" Amy asked finally, after a few minutes of silence.

"Nope, I'm staying home all weekend with you." Maya said, without even looking up from her paper. Only then did Amy notice that her mother was also dressed in a sweat suit with her hair pulled back in a messy ponytail. Amy groaned as she pulled herself out of the chair and limped over to the fridge to get some breakfast.

"Sore?" Maya asked absently and Amy groaned again.

"I feel like I've been run over by a Mack truck, rolled down a hill and then pelted with stones." Amy answered and Maya's lips turned up with a hint of a smile. Her eyes however remained dark and guarded.

"I don't suppose you want to talk about it." Maya said lightly, letting it come out as a statement more than a question. Amy just gave her a pointed look and reached into the cupboard for a bowl.

"That's what I thought. So until we figure this out, you're not allowed to go back to karate." Maya said and Amy slammed the bowl down on the counter.

"You can't ground me again! I didn't do anything!" Amy protested, anger flashing in her eyes.

"I'm not grounding you, I'm protecting you. Someone is hurting you and you keep telling me that it's from karate class. So until I find out who it is, I'm not about to let you go back there and get hurt again." Maya explained, her voice even and emotionless.

"But mom, the tournament is next weekend! I already paid and everything!" Amy whined, bringing her breakfast to the table, but remaining standing.

"Too bad." her mother said, turning back to her paper. Amy pouted as she ate her cereal and tried to come up with ways to change her mother's mind. Maya seemed completely unfazed by her daughter's anger as she calmly finished her coffee and brought her cup to the sink.

"Kyle's coming over later to spend New Year's Eve with us. You might as well pick a movie for us to watch." Maya suggested as she left the kitchen and disappeared in her room. Amy pushed away her bowl and crossed her arms. She would have to talk to Kyle tonight, because their secret was going to have to come out. And soon.

❧

"Your mom was asking me all kinds of questions when I came in." Kyle whispered to Amy as they sat side by side on the couch. Maya had just left to make more popcorn and they had paused the movie.

"She wanted to know if I saw someone hurting you at karate. She was being really pushy, too. She knows that something is going on." Kyle continued and Amy rolled her eyes.

"Of course she does. My mom's not stupid Kyle, she's going to figure it out eventually. She already grounded me from karate." Amy told him, keeping her voice low. Kyle's eyes bugged out of his head and he sat up straighter.

"But the tournament's this weekend!" he exclaimed, forgetting to be quiet.

"Shhh!! I told her that, but she doesn't care." Amy explained and Kyle let his head fall back against the cushions.

"This sucks! How long are you grounded for this time?" he asked, more quietly. Amy shrugged and looked back at the television screen.

"Until I tell her what's really going on." Amy answered and Kyle groaned.

"You're not going to tell her are you?" he asked, looking slightly worried. Amy started to shake her head, but stopped when a bowl of popcorn appeared in front of her.

"Tell me what?" Maya asked, handing her daughter the bowl and going to sit next to Kyle.

"What happens at the end of the movie. We saw it already." Amy answered, after a second's hesitation. Maya shook her head and turned back to the TV screen.

"You wouldn't want to ruin the surprise." she mumbled sarcastically and Amy swallowed hard. Kyle sat stiffly between the two women, unsure of what to do. Amy started the movie again and stared straight ahead as did her mother. Kyle sighed and sank lower into the cushions. He felt awful for what he was doing to his best friend's family, but he was too terrified to do anything about it. Life could really suck sometimes.

❧

Maya was glad when Monday finally rolled around and she went back to work. She and Amy had spent the entire day Sunday ignoring each other and it was really starting to get on her nerves. She sat down at her desk and waited for James to get off the phone. The minute he hung up, she pounced.

"So, what did you find out?" she asked him, leaning forward with her elbows on her desk.

"We ran everyone we could affiliate with the club and they all came up clean." he said and Maya sat back in her chair and blew out a frustrated sigh.

"But… I managed to find out that the sensei, Greg Boltis was picked up once for assault before being released the next day. He was never formally charged. I'm trying to track down the officer that was working the case, but it could take a while because she's not with the same unit anymore." James said and Maya perked up considerably.

"Let me know as soon as you find something. Now maybe we should get to work before I get myself fired." Maya said, when she noticed the captain watching her from his office.

"So we're up to four victims. We talked to their coaches and their parents and the girls had discussed quitting way in advance and they all parted on good terms. We're still checking out Gabriella Fabiolo's coach because that guy seemed to be at least a little miffed that his star athlete up and left him. So far, he seems to have an airtight alibi." James explained and Maya shuffled through the four files on her desk. Four beautiful smiling faces stared up at her from the folders and she couldn't help but feel a little guilty for taking a weekend off when their killer was still out there.

"And we haven't had any hits with the black belt theory." Maya added tapping her pencil on the top file.

"The only girl who even took karate is Fabiolo. The families of the other girls denied them even having a passing interest in the sport." James added.

"So we're back to square one." Maya said with a sigh.

"Yep." James answered, shutting the folder on his desk and crossing his arms.

"Great." Maya said sarcastically, crossing her own arms.

"I guess we're going to be here a while."

☙

Maya made a point of coming home relatively early on the days that Amy had karate to make sure that she wouldn't sneak out. It was awful to have to spy on her daughter, but she just couldn't afford to trust her with something this important. On Tuesday, Amy was working and Maya went out with Harry. They picked Amy up after work and she was silent all the way home. Maya again tried to talk to her, but all she managed to do was make Amy hide in her room. By Friday, they were both stretched to the limit. At a loss for what else to do, Maya arranged a meeting for Amy with one of her coworkers. She picked Amy up at school and the teen was silent all the way to the station.

"What are we doing here?" Amy grumbled when Maya parked the car and got out. Maya didn't answer right away; she just pushed her daughter ahead of her. Amy shrugged away from her mother's touch and marched ahead on the way to the elevator. When Maya pushed the button for the fourth floor, Amy looked over at her with a frown.

"Where are we going mom?" she asked again.

"We're meeting someone." Maya said vaguely. Amy followed her down the hallway without another word. When she saw the plaque on the door however, Amy stopped dead in her tracks.

"You're sending me to a shrink!" Amy exclaimed incredulously. Maya stopped with her hand on the doorknob and turned to look at her daughter. Amy's face was a mask of hurt and anger. Maya turned away quickly, unable to look at her daughter like that.

"He's a friend. I just want you to talk to him." Maya said quietly.

"No way! I can't believe you!" Amy said loudly, taking a step back.

"Don't make a scene Amy. Just go in there and talk to him. It's not that complicated." Maya said, losing patience. Amy shook her head in disbelief. Squaring her jaw, she marched past her mother and yanked open the door.

"Fine, but you're not coming in here. Why don't you go do some of that detective work you love so much? I'll meet you in your office when I'm done. I don't want you with me." Amy said venomously before disappearing into the office. Maya felt as though she had been slapped. Her daughter had never spoken to her that way. She just had to keep telling herself that this was in Amy's best interest. Otherwise, she would just back off to keep her daughter happy like she usually did. And that might do more harm than good. Because as much as Maya hated having her daughter angry with her, she hated seeing her daughter hurt even more.

&

Amy sat with her arms crossed as she waited for the shrink to say something. She thought this was an absolute waste of time and she was furious with her mother for arranging something like this behind her back. Why couldn't Maya just leave her alone like she usually did? When Amy had refused to answer most of his questions, the shrink had lapsed into silence. It was as if he were just waiting for Amy to break the silence on her own. Well she was more than ready to show him just how stubborn she could be.

"Do you love your mother?" he asked finally and Amy looked up, surprised.

"I did until half an hour ago." Amy said sarcastically.

"Do you think she loves you?" he asked and Amy looked at him curiously. Now that she had started talking, she couldn't very well revert to the silence that had seemed so safe.

"Well yeah, she's my mom." Amy said with a frown, wondering what he was getting at.

"Is she a good mother?" he asked next and Amy looked down at the name plate on his desk. Andrew Long, it read and the name bounced around in Amy's brain as she thought about his question.

"I already answered that." Amy said, avoiding the question.

"No, you said you loved her, not that she was a good mother. They are not the same." he said calmly and Amy scratched her head absently as she thought about it. She wanted to just say yes and get it over with, but her anger was pushing her to look deeper.

"I don't know." Amy said finally and Andrew nodded as if this were the most important answer in the world.

"Does she hurt you?" he asked next, as if this were the most normal thing in the world.

"No way!" Amy said, forgetting for a moment that she was supposed to be a difficult patient. She had planned to ignore him, but his questions were starting to get to her. As angry as she was at her mother, she didn't want someone getting the idea that Maya was abusing her.

"But you don't think she's a good mother." he told her, as if stating the obvious.

"I never said that. Besides what does this have to do with anything?" Amy said, getting more upset.

"If she doesn't abuse you, then why do you think she's a bad mother?" he asked, totally ignoring her outburst.

"I don't think she's a bad mother. You're twisting my words. She just doesn't act like a mother." Amy said, shifting uncomfortably in her chair as she tried to fix this impression she had mistakenly created of her mother.

"What is a mother supposed to act like?" Andrew asked, leaning back in his chair and clasping his hands together.

"Well, they're supposed to have rules and they're supposed to get mad at you when you swear. They're supposed to cook nice dinners and bake cookies when you have a sleep-over. They're supposed to embarrass you in front of your friends, because they just have to say they love you even if it's really not cool. They're supposed to help you with your homework and help you when you have a problem. And they're not supposed to date loser guys. They're supposed to rub your back when you cry and tell you everything is going to be alright. And they're supposed to know everything that's going on in your life even without you telling them because moms are like that." Amy said and then she sank deeper in her chair, feeling like she had said too much.

"And your mom's not like that?"

"I didn't mean to say that all moms are like that. I know they're all different. It's just that sometimes my mom… well she's more like a friend than a mom. And that's cool, because most of the time she's really fun. But…" Amy said and wanted to take it back. She was painting an ugly picture of her mother and that wasn't her intention.

"But sometimes you just wish she was different." He finished for her and she nodded.

"Sometimes I just wish she was more like the soccer moms who go to all the games and always know the score and make you study really hard for your test because they know that you can do better and who want you to become an astronaut or a doctor, because they know you're the smartest and who know all your favorite things and who tuck you in at night even though you're too old, who always know just the right thing to say to make you feel better, every time."

"Instead of…" Andrew pressed.

"Instead of a mother who goes to the bar dressed in skimpy bar clothes, because she wants to feel young. Or a mom that all the guys in your class want to make out with, or who thinks that it's okay if she works every night because she left a note on the kitchen table. A mother who hates talking about anything serious and who never said 'be careful'. A mother who is so strong and tough that it makes you feel like you have to hide it if you're scared or hurt. A mother who is so beautiful that you won't even bother wearing makeup or dressing up because she's the only one anyone will ever see anyways. Who likes all the wrong guys and doesn't think that it bothers you. Who doesn't even realize that you're trying as hard as you can to make her proud of you. Who thinks religion is a waste of time and doesn't realize that it's her job to teach you the things that can't be taught at school." Amy passionately, saying the things that she had been thinking for a while, but had never dared say.

"You're not recording this or anything are you?" she asked, realizing how bad it would be if her motd it. He just shook his head absently and continued writing on the note pad in front of him.

"You can't tell her any of this. She'd freak. I shouldn't have said anything. She's not a bad mother at all. I was just pissed at her because she made me come here." Amy babbled trying to fix the mess she had talked herself into. Realizing that it was pointless, she abruptly stood up.

"Is that why you can't tell her who's hurting you?" Andrew asked finally. His voice was still calm and not at all judgmental.

"No." Amy said, just wanting to get out of there.

"Can I go now?" she asked, edging towards the door.

"You can leave whenever you want, but if you ever need to talk, you know where my office is." he said and Amy quickly mumbled her thanks and left the office. She hurried down the hallway towards her mother's office, wanting to get as far away as possible from the nice man with his prying questions. She was flushed with guilt the moment she saw her mother sitting alone at her desk with her head in her hands and papers scattered across her desk. The office was deserted and Maya seemed to be deep in thought as she didn't even hear Amy walk in. Her head snapped up when Amy touched her shoulder lightly. She started to smile then stopped when she saw the look on Amy's face.

"I guess it didn't go well." she remarked, wincing slightly.

"No. Can we just go home now?" Amy asked the anger coming back full force.

"Yeah, just let me get my things." Maya said, impassive. Amy sat at James' desk and crossed her arms to show her mother just how angry she really was. Maya hurriedly packed up all the folders and shrugged into her coat. She logged off her computer and got to her feet. Her heels clicked as she strode purposefully towards the door.

"Let's go." she said over her shoulder, not even looking back. Amy followed like she usually did and the conversation she had with Dr. Long came back to her in bits. She stared at her mother's back and acknowledged that maybe she was more bothered by her mother's actions than she usually let on.

Chapter 9

Maya went to work early Saturday morning and the moment she heard the front door close Amy jumped out of bed. She pulled on some clothes and quickly packed a bag with her karate stuff and some snacks and water bottles. Pulling her coat on, she slung the bag over her shoulder and carefully placed a hand-written note on the kitchen table, just like her mother often did. Amy left the apartment and locked the door behind her, hurrying out into the frigid January air. She could see her breath coming out in small puffs as she hurried over to Kyle's house. He met her at the end of the driveway and together they walked to the bus stop.

"Are you sure your mom's okay with this?" Kyle asked as they boarded the bus and looked for an empty seat. Amy thought it best not to answer. After a few minutes of silence, Amy decided to tell Kyle about Dr. Long.

"She sent you to a shrink? Why?" Kyle asked, looking totally perplexed.

"Because she thinks I'm going crazy. I don't know what made her do it, but it sure wasn't very fun. I gave the doctor an earful though." Amy said with a grin. Kyle laughed and nodded.

"Awesome." he said and Amy felt better.

"So in three hours, we'll be competing in our first karate tournament. How does that make you feel?" Kyle asked in an exaggerated tone. Amy laughed and put her hand to her forehead.

"I'm *so* nervous." she said, playing along as he pretended to be her shrink.

"So you're nervous. Why do you think that is?" he asked, trying to look serious even though his eyes twinkled mischievously.

"Because I'm afraid I'm gonna get my ass kicked." Amy answered and Kyle let himself grimace before returning to his overly compassionate and phoney façade.

"Yes, but how does that make you feel?" he asked again and Amy swatted him playfully.

"Enough with the shrinking! I had more than enough of that yesterday with Dr. Long prying into my brain." Amy protested and Kyle burst out laughing. He held off for all of five seconds; until he absolutely couldn't help himself.

"And how does that make you feel?"

⁂

"Andrew! I've been trying to track you down all day. How did it go with Amy yesterday?" Maya asked her friend when he stepped into the elevator with her and James. They were on their way back from lunch and were headed to their office to regroup. The morning interviews hadn't gone well. They were making absolutely no progress in the case and Maya was starting to get discouraged.

"Maybe we should talk in my office. Do you have few minutes?" Andrew said, glancing at his watch. Maya was surprised, but tried not to show it as she glanced at James. He nodded to her and she followed Andrew out of the elevator on the fourth floor.

"I won't be long. Tell the others that I'll be right up." Maya told her partner before hurrying to join Andrew as he unlocked the door to his office. He ushered her in and she slipped into the chair in front of his desk, trying not to appear as nervous as she actually was.

"Did she tell you who was hurting her?" Maya asked impatiently. Andrew sat behind his desk and leaned forward.

"No, but she didn't deny that she was being hurt either." Andrew answered and Maya sat back, relaxing slightly.

"Well that's something at least." she acknowledged and Andrew watched her with a serious look on his face.

"Yes, but that's not what I wanted to talk to you about." Andrew said quietly and Maya immediately tensed up.

"Amy didn't want me to tell you this, but I think it's important that you know." He started and Maya's heart started beating faster.

"Your daughter had a lot to say about you, actually. It's obvious that she loves you very much, but I think the reason that she can't talk to you about what's going on is that she's afraid of what you're going to think. She feels inferior to you Maya. She's put you up on this pedestal and she's convinced that she can never be as good as you, as pretty, as strong. She's afraid and that makes her feel weak. She said that she thinks of you as more of a friend than a mother and that bothers her." he said as gently as possible. He wanted his friend to know what she was up against, but he didn't want to overwhelm her.

"That's ridiculous! I can be her mother and her friend, that doesn't change anything." Maya protested, feeling like he was attacking her style of parenting.

"It does though, because you don't tell a friend the same things that you tell a parent. She feels like you're emotionally closed off. There are many things that she feels she can't tell you because she thinks you don't want to talk about them. That's partly why she feels so alone." he continued and Maya felt heat rush up her cheeks.

"I do work a lot, but I'm still there for her. We talk all the time. She tells me everything." Maya told him, feeling guilty and a little embarrassed.

"I'm not criticizing you, Maya. I know how hard you work, I just think it's really important that you understand what Amy's feeling right now. It might be the only thing that will help you get through to her." he said, trying to calm her down. Maya nodded and took a deep breath.

"What else did she say?" Maya asked, steeling herself against the answer that she didn't really want to hear.

"She thinks that you're beautiful, but she doesn't think she is, that's why she acts like a tomboy so much, because if she doesn't try to be beautiful, then she won't be disappointed. She compares herself to you in everything and she's convinced that she doesn't measure up. All she wants is to make you proud and she feels like it isn't working." Maya forced herself to listen, even though she wanted to press her hands to her ears to stop the words. She closed her eyes and put her head in her hands as she pictured her daughter as she had looked the day before, so hurt and angry.

"I had no idea…" Maya started, trailing off when the lump in her throat prevented her from speaking.

"I know. She does a very good job of hiding her feelings. It took me a while to get her to open up. I think she was as surprised as you when the words came out of her mouth." Andrew said soothingly.

"She feels like she doesn't fit into your life. You have your job and your friends and she mentioned you going out and dressing up. She talked about the guys you like and she feels like you don't care about what she thinks about any of it. She never said 'we' or mentioned the two of you doing anything together. The way she sees it, you're both living separate lives and she wants to jump into yours because she's lonely, but she doesn't want to get in the way. She doesn't quite know where she belongs. She talks tough and she pretends to be confident to cover it up, and it probably works most of the time." he said and Maya swallowed hard.

"What am I supposed to do?" Maya asked in a small voice.

"Talk to her. Tell her how much you love her and how much you want her. She's almost at the same age you were when you had her so she knows what you had to give up to keep her. It wouldn't surprise me if she felt guilty about that." Andrew added and Maya groaned.

"And here I was bragging that my daughter was beautiful and perfect and happy." Maya muttered.

"She still is. She just needs to hear you say that once in a while." Andrew said with a smile. Maya stood up and raked a hand through her hair. She felt numb and knew there was no way she could concentrate on work.

"Thanks Andrew." she said, absently as she left his office. She walked back to her office as if in a daze and sat down heavily in her desk chair. James was talking to a few of their co-workers nearby and looked at her questioningly.

"You okay?" he asked her and she nodded, waving him off. She took a few minutes to compose herself and then she joined the guys. She perched on the edge of one of the desks and listened as they outlined a plan.

"Guys, I've really got to get home. Is there any way you could handle this without me?" Maya asked, suddenly feeling exhausted.

"Are you sure you're alright?" James asked again.

"I'm fine. I just really need to go home." Maya said, more forcefully. The guys all nodded and agreed they would cover for her. Maya eagerly grabbed her coat and left, leaving even her files behind. She needed some time away from work. She needed some time with her daughter.

&

Amy stopped near the phone booth at the Tim Horton's and thought about calling her mother. Now that they were in Guelph, there wasn't much her mother could do to stop her. She shrieked when she felt something cold smash into the back of her head and trickle down her back.

"You didn't!" Amy exclaimed as she tried to clear away the snow before it all melted and ran down her back. Kyle was already making another snowball when Amy turned to glare at him. She couldn't help but laugh however, when he was pelted in the arm by a snowball thrown by Charles.

"Get him!" Amy shouted and snowballs started flying. The guys all got into the game and there was a hard fought battle before they all piled into the Tim Horton's laughing.

"You should've seen your face when I got you with that first snowball!" Kyle told Amy and she stuck her tongue out at him.

"That was pretty good." Charles agreed, still laughing himself.

"Fine, I'll admit it. It was a good shot. But who's the one that ate the snowball in the face?" she asked and Kyle blushed.

"That would be me." he said, looking sheepish.

"I win." Amy said happily and Kyle's eyes narrowed, even though he was still grinning.

"We'll just have to wait and see who the winner is in the end." he said and Amy flexed her muscles, trying to look mean. Kyle did the same and everyone laughed.

"Oh no, we'd better watch out for those two." Dave said sarcastically, pretending to be afraid.

"You got that right! Because we're lean mean fighting machines!" Kyle said and Dave chuckled.

"If you say so."

છ

Maya saw the note as soon as she came into the apartment.

"Shit!" she muttered as she dropped the note back onto the table. She hurried out of the apartment, quickly locking the door behind her. She ran back down to her car and sped off as she flipped open her phone and dialled information.

"Guelph" she said into the phone, speeding across an intersection.

"I need the number for the University of Guelph." she said and then fumbled for a pen as she skidded to a stop at a red light. She wrote down the number and then smashed her hand on the steering wheel in frustration.

"If he doesn't kill you Amy, I will." Maya said to no one as she pressed on the accelerator.

༄

By the time they got dressed and met in the gym, Kyle was nervous. He wiped his sweaty palms on his *gi* pants and went to sit with the others from their club in the bleachers.

"You should find somewhere to stretch and practice your *kata* because that's going to be first." Sensei said and everyone left. Kyle looked around and was awed by the spectacle in front of him. There were four rings in use all at the same time. The younger kids were competing first and it was almost overwhelming to see so much activity at the same time. There were people everywhere and the gym was filled to capacity. Kyle and Amy ended up escaping to the hallway, were they finally found an empty spot. They stretched quickly and practiced their *kata* before returning to the bleachers. Amy kept telling Kyle to hurry up because she was afraid they would miss the announcement for their divisions. Luckily, they wouldn't be competing against each other because guys and girls were in separate categories. So all Kyle had to worry about were the white, yellow and orange belt guys. Piece of cake. Kyle gulped when he saw a tall orange belt guy pass by and he revised that thought. Maybe this was a bad idea after all.

༄

Maya looked at the clock on the dash and forced herself to slow down. Getting pulled over for speeding wasn't going to help Amy at all. Besides, she needed a little more time to figure out what she was going to say to Amy when she found her. She was furious that her daughter had left without telling her and what's more, she was on her way to compete in a karate tournament when Maya specifically told her that she couldn't go. But the long ride in the car only made Maya think more about what Andrew had told her. How could she not notice that her daughter was feeling so mixed up? She saw her daughter every day, it wasn't like they were strangers. Andrew had to be wrong. Maya leaned over and looked at herself in the rear view mirror. She was nothing special, how could her daughter possibly think that she didn't measure up? Every time Maya thought about Amy, she couldn't help but smile. Her daughter was beautiful and smart and strong, no matter what Amy believed. Maya sighed as she turned off the highway. Andrew was right about one thing, she and Amy really needed to talk and this time, she wouldn't take no for an answer.

Amy's group got called first and she practically ran to the mat on the left where the other girls were gathering. There weren't any novice girls from her club competing and Amy was curious to see what her competition would look like. Kyle and Sensei were watching from the bleachers along with the rest of the gang who had yet to compete. Amy counted seven other girls who would be competing and three of them were orange belts while three others had yellow belts with an orange stripe. Only one of the girls was a white belt and she looked about as nervous as Amy felt. They all bowed in and then the first girl was called to do her *kata*. Her *kata* looked flawless and Amy saw her chances of winning flying out the window. The next girl stumbled slightly once and Amy felt a little better. Until her name was called. She willed her legs to stop shaking as she walked to the center of the ring and bowed to the judges. She announced the name of her *kata* with as much confidence as she could muster and then launched into action. Thirty seconds later, she was again bowing to the judges as she finished. She hadn't messed up once and she could barely contain her excitement as she left the mat and sat down to wait for her score. Once everyone was done, they announced the winners, who just happened to be two of the orange belts and one of the second level yellow belts. Amy hung her head in defeat and went back to the bleachers to sit with the others.

"You did great!" Sensei said, clapping her on the back.

"But I didn't win." Amy said glumly and he laughed.

"Nope. That sucks doesn't it." he said and Amy smiled despite knowing that she should be upset.

"Yeah it does." she said, realizing that losing to people who were a few levels ahead of her wasn't the end of the world. Kyle's group had already been called while she was presenting and now she searched for him in the ring to the right. There were two guys from their club competing in the novice men's division. Brandon, the orange belt from their club was presenting his *kata* to the judges. He did very well and Amy grimaced as she surveyed Kyle's competition. Most of the guys were big and although there were two white belts and three yellow belts present, the two orange belts looked very intimidating. Amy felt herself tense up when she saw Kyle walk to the middle of the mat and bow. She heard him announce his *kata* from where she sat, which was a good thing, and then he started.

"He looks strong. That's good." Sensei commented as Kyle made the first turn and completed another block.

"See how his back leg is bent? And he bobs up with each move. It's important to stay at the same level when you're moving." Sensei added, always ready to teach his students. Amy nodded as she took in his advice and made a mental note to tell Kyle later. Kyle finished his *kata* and bowed to the judges. Amy thought she heard her name being called and looked around quickly. Not seeing anyone that she knew, she again focused on Kyle's ring to see what his scores would be.

"They were tough on him!" Sensei said with a low whistle when he saw Kyle's scores. Amy winced, but couldn't help feeling relieved. She would never have lived it down if Kyle had finished higher than her.

"Amy!" she heard her name being called again, this time much closer. She whirled around to see her mother standing close by.

"Mom! What are you doing here?" Amy asked, her eyes opening wide and t drumming in her chest.

"I could ask you the same question." Maya said, looking furious. Amy felt sweat break out just as she heard her division being called for *kumite*. She took a deep breath and got ready to stand up to her mother.

"That's me. I'm going to finish what I started." Amy said and started riffling through her bag for her new *kumite* mitts and her mouth guard. Her mother stood watching her with her mouth hanging open, not quite believing that Amy would ignore her.

"Mom, this is my sensei, Greg Boltis. This is my mother, Maya Brendan." Amy introduced quickly and Greg shook Maya's hand before following Amy down to the ring on the right where Kyle's group had just finished their *kata* competition.

"Kick some ass Amy." Kyle said as she passed by.

"I'll try. Your *kata* was good by the way." Amy answered and Kyle smiled at her before going back up to the bleachers. If he was surprised to see Maya there, he didn't let on. He just sat next to her and adjusted his glasses as if that would help him to better see the match.

"*Zanchin* means continued presence. You have to stay engaged during the entire match. Finish your techniques and watch your opponent. Never let your guard down even when the match is stopped. Now remember what we practiced: one, two, three. Always follow up with a second and third or even fourth technique. You can do it." Sensei said and Amy nodded and joined the girls standing at the edge of the mat. They bowed in and then were separated into two groups. Amy was told to put on a red belt and she clumsily tied the belt with shaking hands. Then she slipped her mouth guard into her mouth and waited for her turn. She was so nervous that her mouth felt as dry as the Kalahari Desert and the fact that her mother had shown up out of nowhere was definitely not helping. The first match was rough with an orange belt girl winning five to two over a yellow belt with an orange stripe. Then Amy's name was called and she panicked. She glanced over at her sensei and she saw him nod at her and mouth *one, two, three*. She nodded vigorously and stepped up to the mat. She bowed and then approached her line. Luckily, she was fighting the lone white belt and the fact that she was likely more experienced than a white belt gave her a much needed boost of confidence. They spent the first thirty seconds at least circling each other, neither one of them wanting to make a move.

"Go Amy!" she heard her sensei yell and she lunged forward, fists flying. The girl blocked her and countered with a kick. Amy blocked and tried another punch that she followed up with a kick. The referee stopped the match and both girls returned to their lines.

"*Shudan Giri, Nihon!*" the referee announced, awarding Amy two points for the kick to the side. Amy felt like she was flooded with energy after that and she easily won the match, getting a few more points and effectively blocking all her opponent's attacks.

"*Aka No Kachi!*" the referee said, announcing red as the winner of the match. Amy shook the other girl's hand, remaining calm even though she was ready to burst with excitement. She practically ran back to her sensei who greeted her with a pat on the back and a wide smile.

"Way to go! I knew you had it in you. But you're not done yet. You've got to do it again and this time I want to see you dig deeper." he said as Amy greedily guzzled some water to keep her gums from sticking together in her dry mouth.

"Watch what she does with her foot." Sensei instructed as they watched the other two orange belts fight each other. The taller of two girls was much bigger, but the shorter one was faster. She was able to change the direction of her kick at the last minute, leaving the tall girl little chance to block. Forty-five seconds and two kicks to the head later, their match was over.

"Two kicks! She won the match with only two kicks!" Amy exclaimed and her sensei nodded.

"Kicks to the head are three points each and they stop the match if you have a six point spread. So remember that. I know you're flexible and you're taller than most of the girls. Kicks to the head will get you ahead fast." he explained and Amy thought about what he said as she stepped back onto the mat for her second match. This time she had to fight the orange belt who had won the first match. Amy gulped as she stood in front of the older girl. She didn't have much time to be nervous however, because the match soon started. In no time, the other girl had accumulated three points and Amy found herself losing. *One, two, three*, she thought to herself before launching an attack. She punched twice before kicking high and fast, just grazing the other girl's ear.

"*Jodan Giri, Sanbon!*" the referee announced as he awarded Amy three points for her kick to the head. They fought for a while longer without anyone getting a point.

"*Hikiwake Encho-Sen*. Tie, next point wins." the referee announced and Amy braced herself for an attack. She decided to wait for her opponent to attack and when she did Amy was ready. She blocked the kick and countered with a punch to the stomach.

"*Ippon, Aka No Kachi!*" came the referee's decision and Amy couldn't help but smile over her victory as she left the mat.

"That was close!" she exclaimed as she reached Greg. Unfortunately, the short orange belt with the wicked kick also won her match and then Amy was facing her in the final match for the gold medal. Amy fought valiantly, but in the end she was no match for the wicked kick. She lost the final match six to two and she gladly accepted her silver medal.

"We'll work on that when we get back home." Sensei said, shaking her hand.

⁊

Maya watched in awe as Amy won one match and then another. She looked strong and sure as she moved around the ring and Maya wondered if she had made the right decision by banning karate. Her daughter was good and with enough practice, she could be really good. Maya saw Amy run back to her sensei after every match. He always had something to say and Maya could see him pointing at the girls in the ring while they were competing. He looked like any other coach, intent on helping his athlete to be victorious. Maya groaned when Amy lost the final match. She had actually though that Amy might win and she knew her daughter would be very disappointed. She watched the sensei's reaction closely and noticed how he tried to cheer Amy up. Maya had expected him to get upset, but that wasn't the case at all. Amy celebrated her near victory with the others for a moment before coming back to the bleachers almost reluctantly. Her sensei had already crossed over to the other ring where Kyle was about to bow in. Maya watched as Amy sat next to her, keeping her eyes down. She calmly placed her mitts and mouth guard back in her duffel bag and then cleared her throat.

"I know you're probably really mad, but-" Amy started but Maya cut her off.

"Yes I am, but we can talk about that later. Now I want to see your medal." Maya said and Amy looked up at her in surprise as if not sure whether to believe what her mother was saying.

"I'm serious. Let me see." Maya said as she reached for the medal that was hanging from her daughter's neck and examined the inscription.

"I really wanted to win though. I wanted to show you that karate wasn't a bad thing and that I was getting good." Amy said with a sigh.

"You did. You were awesome in that ring and you don't need a gold medal to prove it. I had no idea you were that good." Maya said and Amy shrugged fingering her silver medal. They didn't say anything more as they both turned to watch Kyle as he stepped into the ring.

☙

Kyle reluctantly handed his glasses over to Sensei and then stepped into the ring. He was terrified and was trying hard not to show it. Amy had made it look so easy that he couldn't possibly back out now without looking like a major wimp. Squaring his shoulders, Kyle got ready to face his opponent. After a few punches and kicks were exchanged, the other guy was winning two to nothing and Kyle was starting to get frustrated. That's why he didn't notice when his opponent swept his foot out from under him. Kyle went down hard on that mat, surprised and afraid. A picture of his father standing over him replaced the face of the orange belt. His anger and helplessness from all the times his father and his druggie friends had hurt him and exploited him gave Kyle a strength he didn't know he had and he bounced back to his feet before his opponent could strike him. He lunged forward and landed a punch to the other guy's face. He was awarded a point and the match resumed. Kyle flew forward with several punches and kicks, eventually getting two more points. He won the match five to three and he was breathing hard by the end.

"That was good, but you need to relax. You'll see more clearly if you're calm." his sensei said, noticing Kyle's anger. Kyle nodded, but couldn't help but feel that this was his chance to get back for all the crap he had taken over the years, not just from his father, but also from Joe Wharton and the kids at school who had taunted him. Kyle pummeled the white belt he fought next and found himself in the finals.

"You'd better watch it, Kyle. If you hit much harder, you're going to get a penalty and you don't want to give away any points. This next guy is good and he's fast, but you can take him." Sensei said and Kyle nodded, not really listening. Kyle got two points right off the bat for his kick to the side, but then he got his first warning for excessive contact when his opponent's head snapped back after Kyle hit him in the face. Kyle backed off a little, but was soon hit with two punches to the stomach that got the other guy two points. His anger flaring up again, Kyle swung hard at the orange belt who blocked his punch, swinging Kyle around so that his back was to his opponent. Kyle kicked back as hard and as high as he could. He felt his foot connect and then he heard the referee calling the match to a halt. Kyle returned to his line, expecting a point and was surprised to see the orange belt on his knees with his hand pressed to his face. The medic ran out and Kyle held his breath. His anger left him all at once and was replaced by a queasy feeling deep inside. The orange belt pulled away from the medic and returned to his line, but looked at Kyle warily. Kyle didn't even hear the referee give him another penalty or award his opponent a point because there was one thought in his head requiring all his attention. He was a bully. Kyle was turning out to be just like his father.

Chapter 10

Kyle's heart just wasn't in it for the rest of the match. His opponent won easily and he had to settle for the silver medal. A gold medal wasn't worth becoming what he was most afraid of. Amy and Maya were silent when he returned to the bleachers.

"Well at least we both almost won." Amy said with forced cheerfulness. Kyle nodded sadly. Maya made a big show of comparing their two silver medals, but Kyle noticed when she looked at him oddly. Kyle wasn't one to get angry easily and he worried that Maya would wonder why he was acting so vicious. Even Amy seemed uneasy around him.

"We should go. It's late and I have to work early tomorrow." Maya said, standing up and searching in her pockets for her car keys.

"I'll go back with Dave. I already asked him for a ride." Kyle said, trying to avoid Maya's gaze. She looked like she was about to argue, but instead she nodded and turned to Amy. Amy shot him an annoyed glance, knowing full well that she was going to get one hell of a lecture from her mother during the long drive home if Kyle wasn't there to run interference. He just shrugged and sat down on the bench, pretending to watch the intermediate guys compete. Amy looked from Kyle to her mother before stalking off towards the doors. When she was gone, Kyle breathed a sigh of relief and then dropped his head into his hands. What had he gotten himself into?

ↄ৲

Maya glanced over at Amy again as she sped along the highway. Amy was slouched low in her seat and was examining her medal for the umpteenth time since they had left the University. She was obviously trying her best to be invisible and Maya knew she would be perfectly happy if neither of them spoke all the way home.

"We need to talk Amy, and I don't want you to blow me off." Maya said quietly. Amy didn't look up. She let the medal fall onto her chest that heaved as she sighed deeply.

"I can't trust you anymore and that scares me. You keep sneaking out and lying to me and I just don't know what I'm supposed to do." Maya said, hazarding a look at her daughter. Amy still didn't look up.

"What was with the note? Were you trying to piss me off?" Maya asked, a little more forcefully.

"It's what you always do." Amy said under her breath. Maya's frown deepened.

"What?" she asked, confused.

"You leave notes on the kitchen table all the time." Amy said matter-of-factly.

"I'm letting you know where I am, Amy. You were letting me know that you ran off. It's not the same thing. You knew I would be worried about you, but you did it anyways." Maya explained, her voice rising.

162

"It is the same! Don't you think I worry too? You're gone all the time and I'm not supposed to worry when you're running after murderers with a gun in the middle of the night, while I stay home alone with one flimsy lock on the door!" Amy exclaimed and Maya gritted her teeth as she considered what her daughter was saying.

"You don't have to worry about me. I'm a big girl and I can take care of myself." Maya said and Amy made a show of staring out the window.

"Whatever." Amy muttered and Maya tightened her grip on the steering wheel and blew out a frustrated breath.

"How am I supposed to take care of you if I don't even know where you are? It's my job to protect you, I'm your mother."

"That's debatable." Amy muttered again, her eyes still glued to the side window and her arms crossed tightly over her chest. Maya's mouth dropped open at her daughter's words. Maybe what Dr. Long had said held more truth than Maya had wanted to believe.

"Why don't you just ground me again and we can get this over with." Amy said in an even voice, sounding older than her sixteen years.

"I don't want to ground you Amy. I hate grounding you. You're really good at karate and I don't want to have to take that away from you. I'm willing to admit that maybe I overreacted when I told you karate was out, but you can't just do whatever you want. We have to get back to some semblance of a normal life. We just can't keep going this way." Maya explained.

"You play fair and I'll play fair." Amy said, looking at her mother out of the corner of her eye.

"That's all I want." Maya conceded, relaxing slightly. They drove in silence for a few minutes before Maya tried again.

"You really were amazing at the tournament today. I was really proud of you." Maya said, catching Amy's eye, long enough to see the hope spring up there.

"Even if I didn't win?" Amy asked, fingering her medal and keeping her head down.

"You won silver and you fought hard. That's good enough for me. It's better than I could do." Maya prayed with each word that she was saying the right thing and she waited to see what Amy's reaction would be. Amy sat up a little straighter and actually turned to look at her mother.

"That girl had a pretty wicked kick though, didn't she?" Amy asked her mother, sounding more like her normal self.

"She sure did. When you learn how to kick like that you'll be unstoppable!" Maya retorted and she saw her daughter puff up a little more. The smile that lit up her face at her mother's confidence in her abilities nearly made Maya whoop with joy. She was finally getting somewhere with her daughter. Now if she could just figure out who was hurting Amy, they could get on with their lives.

ೞ

Kyle thanked Dave for the ride and waved as the car pulled away from the curb. He hoisted his bag onto his back and headed for the front door. The exhilaration of the day was dying a little now that he was back in his everyday nightmare. Kyle walked into the house and found his father passed out on the couch in front of the television set, surrounded by beer bottles, shot glasses and syringes. He dropped in front of Ken and checked to make sure he was still breathing. Satisfied that his father was alive, Kyle watched him for a moment and tried to remember a time when his father had been normal. He remembered something vague about a ball and a park, but nothing to suggest that his father had ever loved him or even cared about him. With a sigh of defeat, Kyle slowly removed his medal from around his neck.

"Look dad. I won a silver medal. It was a great match too. I nearly took off the guy's head." Kyle told his father's unconscious form. Kyle closed his eyes and pretended that his father was more like Amy's mom, who actually cared enough to come to the tournament, even if she was pissed.

"Next time I'll win the gold dad, you'll see." Kyle continued, pretending that his father wasn't lying in a drug and alcohol induced coma. Pretending that his father was proud of him. Pretending that his father actually knew he was alive.

✂

"Okay, here's the deal. You can go to karate tonight and I'll work late, but we will both be home by eight o'clock. No notes. No excuses." Maya said Monday morning while she drank her coffee. Amy was eating breakfast and she looked up in surprise.

"You mean it?" Amy asked, looking hopefully at her mother.

"Yeah. No lying either." she added and Amy held up her hands, nodding vigorously.

"Deal, totally." she agreed happily and Maya smiled. She shrugged into her jacket and grabbed her keys off the counter. She downed the remainder of her coffee and then walked over to where Amy was sitting.

"Good. I'll see you later. I love you." Maya said, bending over to kiss the top of Amy's head before hurrying out the door. Amy stared at the door for a few minutes after her mother left, wondering what had just happened. Not only was it weird that her mother had changed her mind about karate and had promised to be home, but she had also *kissed* Amy goodbye. She never kissed Amy.

"I love you too." Amy said softly to the closed door. She finished her cereal with a new resolve. She would do her best not to piss off her mother any more than she already had. She just hoped nothing would happen to change the tentative trust she and her mother were trying to rebuild.

ↄ

"I've got good news and bad news." James said the minute Maya sat down at her desk. She lifted her eyebrows questioningly and James slid a folder towards her.

"There's been another attack and this time, he finished the job. He seems to have gone back to his old habits. This time the girl really fits his profile and he killed her." James explained and Maya shook her head.

"What's the good news?" she asked, still reeling from the fact that another young girl was dead because they were failing to catch a killer who had been on the loose for over a month.

"I tracked down the officer that worked your sensei's case and she's going to make sure that the file gets to me by the end of the day." James said and Maya nodded. At least it was something.

"Andrea Warner is twenty-two years old and she was in her fourth year at the University of Toronto. She was apparently beaten to death. Her body was found in an

166

alley outside her apartment building." James explained as Maya flipped through the chart.

"Why weren't we called to the scene?" she asked, annoyed.

"Because the local guys thought they could handle it and they didn't notice the pattern. It was their captain that finally called ours about an hour ago."

"Great, well let's get over to the crime scene and see what we can salvage." Maya suggested, reaching for her coat.

"Perfect, then we can swing by the school and question her friends and her teachers." James added and Maya nodded, leading the way out of the office.

☙

The crime scene had already been processed by the time they got there and they spent the rest of the day canvassing the school. They spoke to Andrea's friends and some of her teachers and they all said that she was a very bright student who was an excellent athlete. She was the best player on the girl's basketball team and her decision to quit the team so suddenly had left them in the lurch.

"Well at least we have a few people with a motive this time." Maya said, trying to look at the bright side of a very bad situation. While James went in to update the captain, Maya started on some paper work so that she would be able to get out of the office on time. She had promised Amy she would be home on time and she intended to keep that promise for once.

"Excuse me, I'm looking for detective Elliott." a woman said, stopping near Maya's desk.

"I'm his partner. Can I help you with something?" Maya asked pleasantly, looking up from the file she was updating.

"You must be detective Brendan. I'm Christine Walton, I was the officer who took in Boltis. I managed to locate his file and I figured I would drop it off in person in case either of you had questions. I don't know how helpful I can be after six years, but I'll try." Christine said pleasantly.

"Please, sit down." Maya said, gesturing to a chair beside her desk as she took the file from Christine.

"Ms. Walton, nice to see you again." James said pleasantly as he came out of the captain's office. He shook her hand and had a seat at his own desk while he waited for Maya to finish reading.

"Please, call me Christine. I read over the file myself to refresh my memory and it certainly wasn't a minor attack." Christine said evenly. Maya slid the file across the desk to her partner without a word. Her face was devoid of color and she looked shocked. James scanned the file quickly and his eyes opened as wide as his partner's.

"Christ, he didn't just assault a man. He broke his elbow and his nose, dislocated his knee, broke three ribs and punctured his spleen. Sounds familiar doesn't it?" James said and Maya felt as if time suddenly slowed, as if he were speaking in slow motion. She blinked at James a few times as she wrestled with the implications of what they had just read.

"Oh my God! The son-of-a-bitch is our murderer and he's probably been hurting Amy too. I was looking for two different guys, but it's been him all along! I talked to him! Amy spent the day with him on Saturday! That bastard could have killed my daughter!" Maya burst out, jumping up from her chair. She took a few deep breaths to try and calm herself as she started for the door.

"Where are you going?" James asked, catching up to her.

"I let her go back to karate." Maya said and James didn't need more of an explanation. He grabbed his partner by the arm and forced her to stop.

"Wait. Let's go talk to Liz and get a warrant first. Then we'll go to Amy's class and pick up Boltis." James reasoned and Maya reluctantly agreed. They hurried down the hall to the office of the attorney for the crown who handled most of their cases and burst in without knocking.

"I'll have to call you back." Liz said into the phone when she saw the looks on their faces. She was a petite woman with blond hair and blue eyes, but she had a spine of steel and a reputation for being merciless when it came to her cases.

"What's so important that you can't bother to knock first?" Liz asked in a slightly irritated voice.

"We have a suspect in our case and we need a warrant now." James said quickly. There was no need to explain which case they were working on. Liz was their friend and besides their case was high profile and everyone knew that they had been working on nothing else for the past month.

"Have you spoken to him yet?" Liz asked with a look of surprise crossing her face.

"No, but he fits the profile perfectly. He has access to the victims, he's a karate instructor and he was arrested for assault six years ago. The victim had similar injuries to those of our vics." James explained and Liz nodded thoughtfully.

"I'll see what I can do." Liz said.

"He's teaching a class right now to a bunch of young adults and my daughter is one of them. We need this warrant and fast." Maya said, trying to instill a sense of urgency in her friend. Liz picked up the phone immediately and dialed a number she knew by heart. She sweet- talked a judge for a while and twenty-five minutes later, Maya and James were speeding towards the college with a signed warrant in their hands.

༄

Amy was glad to be back at karate. Everyone congratulated her and Kyle on their near wins and the mood was light at class. They ended up playing games for the first half hour that doubled as warm-ups. Then Sensei decided that it would be fun to try something new. He showed them how to do a flying side kick just like in the movies. Everyone laughed hysterically as they tried to copy the move. Amy ran and jumped into the air, her side kick looking more like a sad attempt at a motocross trick than a karate move. Kyle's was even worse, he somehow ended up in a heap on the ground and Amy was laughing so hard that she couldn't even help him up. She was pulling him up to his feet when they heard a commotion at the other end of the gym. She was confused when she saw James and her mother talking to her sensei. Sensei Charles had walked over to help and the others were either still practicing or watching the scene unfold. Amy hurried towards the group and stopped dead when she saw her mother pull out her handcuffs. By the time Amy reached her mother, James was reading her sensei his rights.

"Mom! What are you doing?" Amy shrieked, shocked and embarrassed.

"Get in the car Amy." was all her mother said.

"He didn't do anything mom! Let him go!" Amy cried, grabbing her mother's arm and trying to wrench it away from her sensei's arms. Greg looked upset, but he stayed silent as Maya finished cuffing him and started to push him towards the door. Maya just shook off her daughter and kept on moving. Amy started to back away and Maya turned to look at her for a moment.

"Amy, just get in the car and we'll talk about this later." Maya called after her daughter as Amy continued to back away from them, shaking her head. She couldn't believe this was happening. Amy ran to the change room and Kyle followed her in, not caring that it was the girl's change room.

"What are we going to do? This is all my fault! I should never have told my mom that I was getting hurt at karate. We have to tell her the truth!" Amy cried as she paced back and forth, her heart in her throat.

"No wait! Just give me enough time to get my stuff and my money and I'll leave tonight." Kyle said and Amy stopped pacing long enough to stare at him.

"You're going to leave now?" Amy asked feeling even more panicked. Kyle nodded solemnly and Amy went to his side.

"You have to tell your mom the truth about everything and I can't be here when that happens. It's the only way Amy." Kyle said quietly. Amy sat down heavily on the bench and Kyle plopped down next to her. They were silent for a moment before Kyle stood up and pulled Amy to her feet.

"We've got to get out of here, before your mom comes looking for you." Kyle said and Amy nodded.

"I'll go back with you." she said and Kyle nodded before slipping out and heading to the men's change room. Amy quickly changed and then slipped out the back door. Kyle met her there and together they snuck around the back of the building until they made it to a bus stop at the other end of the campus. They boarded a bus that would take them home and Amy couldn't help but feel sad as she realized that this would be the last time that she and Kyle would ride the bus together. What was she supposed to do without her best friend?

എ

Once they had Greg Boltis safely in the car, Maya ran back into the college to find her daughter. A quick search proved futile when Amy was nowhere to be found. She stomped back outside and slipped into the car next to her partner. He raised an eyebrow quizzically when he saw that Maya was alone, but she just shook her head and he started driving. They hauled Boltis into the station and closed him up in an interrogation room.

"I'm telling you! I didn't do anything!" he said forcefully for the tenth time.

"Nice try, but we know what you did to those girls." James said as Maya stood near the door with her arms crossed. James showed Boltis pictures of the dead girls and he looked horrified as he turned his head away, not wanting to see the photos.

"I definitely didn't do that. I didn't even know those girls!" he protested.

"They were all killed by someone who was highly trained in martial arts. Wouldn't you say that you qualify?" James tried again.

"Look, I would never touch anyone and certainly not a young girl!" Greg yelled, trying to get through to the detectives. Maya strode forward and dropped new pictures in front of him. They were the pictures she had taken of Amy's bruises. She shoved a smiling picture of Amy at Christmas with her black eye shining prominently in Greg's face.

"Then what do you call this? Amy said you hit her during a drill. She's claiming it was an accident because she's obviously scared of you." she demanded, angrily. She wanted to kill the bastard for hurting her little girl.

"I never hit Amy. I've been teaching karate for ten years, I have more control than that." Greg said, finally starting to understand what was going on.

"Why don't you tell us about the last time you were arrested?" James demanded, placing a restraining hand on Maya's arm. She forced herself to step back from Boltis as she waited for his answer.

"I wasn't formally charged. That man tried to kidnap my daughter. I turned around for one second at the mall and she was gone. I chased the man out an emergency exit. He had my two year-old in his arms and she was screaming for me. What was I supposed to do?" Greg demanded, pain evident in his eyes as he relived his own nightmare.

"You broke his elbow, his nose and three ribs, you dislocated his knee and you punctured his spleen. Doesn't that seem a little excessive to you?" James asked, reading out of the file in front of him.

"Fine, maybe I lost it, but he had my baby girl and I wasn't about to let him get away." Greg said, not sounding at all sorry for what he had done. Maya became more and more confused as she listened. He didn't sound like a man who would murder girls for fun. The look on his face when he had seen the pictures had almost been enough to convince her. She had interviewed enough suspects to know that they almost always lied and were usually very convincing, but something about this one was wrong. She signaled to James and left the room. James followed her out.

"Can you finish up with him? Something's not right, I'm going to try to find Amy and talk to her again. Maybe now that we arrested her sensei, she'll be ready to talk." Maya explained, her brow furrowed as she tried to figure out what she was missing.

"Sure. Let me know what she says." James told his partner, even though he knew that she wasn't listening. Maya was already on her way out the door.

❧

Amy stayed behind Kyle as he pulled open the door to his house and peered inside. His father was nowhere in sight, so they hurried up the stairs to Kyle's room before he could cause them any trouble. Kyle turned the knob and pushed on the door. It swung open halfway, but stopped as it smashed against something. Kyle frowned and slipped in through the crack. Amy came in behind him and he heard her suck in her breath sharply. It looked like the Tasmanian Devil had been through his room. His drawers had been yanked out of the dresser and their contents were in piles on the ground, his mattress had been pulled off his bed and flipped upside down and now lay partially blocking the doorway. His desk drawers had obviously been rummaged through and everything that had once been in his closet was now strewn about the room. Kyle picked his way through the mess and sank down to his knees next to the desk. The bottom drawer had been ripped out and the video tapes that had been there had been thrown in a pile nearby. Kyle riffled through the videos and picked one up, snapping open the plastic case.

"No! This can't be happening!" he groaned, letting the case fall to the ground. He pulled his knees up to his chest and let his head fall onto them. He felt a hand on his shoulder, but ignored it. He knew men weren't supposed to cry, but he felt so trapped at that moment that he couldn't think of anything else to do.

"Is it all gone?" Amy asked gently. Kyle nodded and he heard her sigh.

"I've been saving up that money for almost a year and now it's gone. What am I supposed to do now?" he asked, swiping at the tears in his eyes.

"Maybe you could stay?" Amy suggested, slowly.

"I can't stay Amy. I bought drugs remember and I can guarantee you that there are drugs all over this house. They would send me to jail. I can't go to jail Amy. If I get beat up that bad at school, just image how it would be in jail. I just can't let that happen." Kyle explained and Amy nodded sadly.

"I know. I just don't want you to go. I'll miss you so much." Amy confessed.

"Me too." Kyle said, looking right into his best friend's eyes. Then he got up and started to pack. He filled up his backpack and a duffel bag, while Amy watched with tears in her eyes. She wanted to be strong for her friend, but she just couldn't stand the thought of him leaving.

"You can't run away with no money. You'll starve. Come back to my apartment with me. I know where my mom has some money stashed for emergencies. This definitely qualifies as an emergency." Amy reasoned, but Kyle shook his head.

"I'm not stealing your mother's money. I've caused her enough trouble already." Kyle said, zipping up his duffel bag. The sound was so final it nearly broke Amy's heart.

"It's not stealing. I'm giving it to you. I'll take some money out of my account tomorrow and I'll replace it. It's no big deal." Amy said, trying her best to convince him.

"Okay, fine. I'll take the money, but I'll pay you back one day. I promise." Kyle conceded, knowing that he had no other choice.

"Will you email me, or something?" Amy asked in a small voice as they sat next to each other for the last time, neither of them ready to move.

"Sure. Once I find a place to stay, I'll look for an internet café or something. If I can't find one, I'll send you a letter to let you know that I'm alright." Kyle said. He knew that Amy would worry until he did, so he made a mental note to reassure her as soon as possible.

"We should go." Kyle said, getting to his feet. Amy's lower lip trembled and he thought she would start to bawl on him, but she sucked it up and stood up as well. He took one last look around his room and then walked out, not daring to look back. Amy followed him and they hurried down the stairs. Kyle couldn't believe that he was actually going to be free of this dungeon that he had been living in for as long as he could remember. He almost felt like smiling as he strode towards the door and his impending freedom.

"Kyle look out!" Amy screamed and Kyle slammed back down to reality. He whirled around in time to get a roundhouse punch to the face. His father looked furious as he attacked his son. Kyle hit back but his punch was blocked effortlessly.

"You're a thief! And you're a liar! You've been stealing my money and saving it for yourself!" Ken yelled as he hit Kyle over and over again.

"I never stole any of your money!" Kyle protested, curling up into a ball on the ground, trying to protect himself from his father's attack. He saw his father's head snap forward as Amy punched him hard. Then he saw a leg come flying when she kicked him in the groin when he turned around. Kyle used the distraction to get to his feet. Ken lunged forward with his head down, barreling right into Amy. She went flying backwards into the coffee table that broke under her weight. Amy stayed down with her eyes closed and Kyle saw red. It was one thing not to stand up for himself, but he wasn't about to let his father hurt his best friend again.

"Leave her alone!" Kyle growled as he flew at his father. He punched and kicked as hard as he could, not even noticing where the strikes landed or if they were doing any damage. His father fell to the floor and Kyle kicked him over and over.

"Stop Kyle, that's enough." Amy said, breaking into his thoughts. It took everything he had in him to pull back. He took a shaky breath and took in the damage he had done. His father was moaning on the floor, clutching his side, blood streaking his face. Amy had pulled herself to her feet and was staring at Kyle with a frightened expression on her face. Kyle took another deep breath and stepped back from his father.

"I should kill you for what you put me through, but I'm not like you. I don't just hurt people for nothing. Goodbye dad." Kyle said in a steely voice. Then he turned his back to his father and picked up his bags. He held his head high as he and Amy walked to the door, leaving his father behind. Kyle had his hand on the knob, when the shot rang out. The sound had barely registered when Amy crumpled at his side.

Chapter 11

Amy fell to the floor, clutching her leg.

"Don't move." Kyle heard his father say as he dropped his bags on the floor. Kyle stayed still, with his hands wide open and out where his father could see them. Amy whimpered beside him and Kyle had to resist the urge to reach down and help her.

"Get away from the door, both of you!" Ken yelled and Kyle half dragged Amy until she was leaning against the other wall.

"Okay, now get over by the TV! I don't want you two trying anything." Ken added, gesturing with his gun. Kyle looked down to see blood already covering Amy's hand and soaking her jeans. She was white as a ghost and looked terrified. He walked slowly over to the television set, watching his father carefully. He didn't want to do anything to piss him off. He didn't care if his father killed him, but he didn't want anything to happen to Amy. He was the one that got her into this mess and he was going to get her out of it. Somehow.

"A thousand bucks! You had almost a thousand bucks stashed in your room and you think I'm going to just let it go? Just like that?" Ken asked angrily. There was a wild look trying to take over his dazed expression and was invading his glazed over, drug-deadened eyes. Kyle thought it better to keep his mouth shut to avoid any more trouble. He needed to find a way to calm his father down before Amy bled to death in his living room.

"You can't possibly think that I'm just going to let you leave. You know too much. You're in too deep. There is no way I'm letting you go." Ken said and Kyle's heart sank deeper. There had to be a way out of this. He just needed to think.

"I should have killed you while I had the chance!" Kyle said, his voice coming out in a vicious rumble. His father just laughed at him and pointed his gun back at Amy's head.

"Too bad you're such a wuss. You don't have the balls to follow through with anything. And you hit like a girl!" Ken said, taunting his son. Kyle gritted his teeth and resisted the urge to say what was on his mind. He just needed to figure out a way to get the gun away from his father. Kyle looked from Amy to Ken and realized that it might not be that easy.

❧

Maya let herself into her apartment and knew right away that her daughter wasn't there. She had expected to see Amy's winter boots by the door, but that wasn't the case. Maya walked through the apartment anyways, just to make sure before heading back out. She drove over to Kyle's even though it wouldn't have taken her any longer to walk there. Maya was just making her way up the driveway when she heard the gun shot. She pulled out her gun and stayed low, running up to the house and flattening herself against the wall next to the door. She waited a moment and then peeked in the window. She saw Ken Thompson lying on the ground with a gun in his hands. He was shouting something, but she couldn't quite make out the words. He was looking towards the door and Maya realized that someone was standing near the door, where she couldn't see them. Her pounding heart nearly stopped in its tracks when she saw Kyle drag Amy away from the door. Maya tore her eyes away from the window and made her way around to the back of the house, where she knew there was a back door.

The back door was locked, but that didn't stop Maya. She had learned how to pick locks when she was ten. She let herself in as quietly as possible and crept towards the front of the house. Maya knew she should call for back up, but she couldn't stand to wait any longer. Closing her eyes, she counted to three and then burst into the living room with her gun raised.

"What the hell is this?!" Ken screamed, struggling to his feet with his gun moving between Maya and Amy.

"You told your fucking mother? You little bitch! I should kill you right now!" Ken yelled, pointing his gun at Amy's head, his hand shaking violently.

"Calm down Ken. Let's just talk about this." Maya said evenly, trying to diffuse the situation. She glanced over at Amy and saw that she was deathly pale, her face pinched in pain. Another furtive glance at her daughter allowed her to see the blood soaking Amy's jeans and dripping onto the floor.

"I want you to keep as much pressure as you can on your leg baby." Maya told her daughter as she trained her gun on Kyle's father. Amy's groan of protest let Maya know that her daughter was actually listening to her for once.

"Come on Ken. Why don't you just let the kids go and we'll talk." Maya suggested. She took in Ken's haggard appearance and the glossy sheen of his eyes and figured he was probably high on drugs and not for the first time either.

"No way! No one's going anywhere!" Ken shouted waving his gun around. He ran a hand through his greasy hair, making it stand on end.

"What do you want Ken?" Maya asked after a moment.

"I want you to go back where you came from!" Ken sputtered and Maya shook her head.

"That's not going to happen. Why won't you let the kids go Ken? Because they know about the drugs?" Maya said on a whim. She waited for a response, praying that she was right.

"Shit!" Ken yelled, scrubbing his face with his hand. Kyle and Amy both stared at her in disbelief and Maya knew that she had guessed right.

"Drugs are one thing, but killing a hostage is another. You don't want to go to jail for killing a kid. Just let them go and-" Maya tried gently. She had to work hard to detach herself from the situation because it was killing her to even think about Amy dying. She kept her eyes on Kyle's father and watched as he digested this information. He let out a string of curse words and stamped his feet angrily, cutting her off.

"I am not going to jail!" he yelled and Maya nodded.

"If you let them go, we can work something out." Maya told him, hoping that he would do the right thing. She took a step closer to Kyle.

"Stop it! Don't fucking move! Kyle, get over here!" Ken yelled and Kyle looked at Maya with fear in his eyes before walking towards his father.

"So what are you going to do? Just wait until Amy bleeds to death? Then I'll kill you myself and you won't have to worry about going to jail!" Maya yelled, panic starting to creep in as she saw Amy's head fall back against the wall.

"Amy! Stay with me, baby!" Maya called over and Amy weakly raised her head again and forced her eyes open.

"Good girl." Maya praised, turning her attention back to Ken Thompson.

"Now listen to me. I'm not here for you. I only came to pick up the kids. Why don't you just put down the gun." Maya said evenly, fighting to remain calm. Just then, they heard sirens in the distance and Ken's head snapped up.

"What the fuck!!" he screamed, looking towards the doorway. Kyle took that opportunity to lunge for the gun. Ken's grip was surprisingly strong and he and Kyle wrestled with the gun. Maya watched helplessly as they fought, not able to get a clear shot off. Finally, Ken won control of the gun and used it to strike Kyle in the head. Kyle went flying into the wall and Maya shot. Ken fell to the ground with a yelp of pain, dropping the gun. Kyle scrambled forward and picked it up, getting to his feet and aiming at his father's head. Ken held his injured shoulder and looked up at his son. Kyle had blood running down his face from a gash on his forehead and pure hatred radiated from him. He shook with anger as he took a step closer to his father, his finger on the trigger.

"Don't Kyle. He's not worth it." Maya said carefully, stepping closer to the boy she had known since he was in kindergarten. Kyle ignored her, his breath coming out in ragged gasps as he towered over his father's cowering figure.

"Give me the gun Kyle. It's over." Maya said, reaching a hand forward while the other kept her own gun aimed at Ken. Kyle hesitated and then slowly lowered the gun, handing it to Maya. Just then, the front door burst open and James swept in with his gun raised, followed by a pair of uniformed cops. One of them immediately radioed for an ambulance while the other walked over to Ken.

"Detective?" he asked questioningly, raising an eyebrow.

"Cuff him." Maya directed, handing both guns to the officer talking on his radio and crossing the room. She dropped down at her daughter's side and smoothed the hair away from her face. Amy's eyes fluttered open for a moment and focused on Maya before closing again.

"Mom" she whispered and Maya felt the tears threaten to overcome her.

"Hold on baby, the ambulance is on its way." Maya pressed down on the wound on Amy's leg to try and stop the blood from flowing. James appeared at her side a moment later and handed Maya a towel that he had swiped from the kitchen. She took it gratefully and pressed it down on her daughter's leg wound.

"You okay buddy?" she heard James ask Kyle, but she didn't hear his response. She glanced over her shoulder to see James holding a similar towel to Kyle's head, his other arm around the shaking boy's shoulders.

"I'm right here Amy." Maya whispered. It felt like hours had passed since they had called the ambulance, but it had probably only been minutes. Maya felt like crying out with relief when she finally heard the sirens. James was beside her in an instant. He scooped Amy up into his arms and carried her outside. They made it to the end of the driveway just as the ambulance squealed to a stop. Two paramedics hopped out and they helped James settle Amy onto a stretcher. Maya got into the ambulance with them and it sped off towards the hospital.

℘

More than an hour later, Maya paced back and forth in the waiting room. Amy had been rushed up to surgery to repair the damage from the bullet. Now, all she could do for her daughter was wait and that was definitely not easy. Maya was used to being in control and her insides twisted up at the thought of someone else making decisions concerning her daughter's life. Even though she wasn't a religious person, Maya prayed that the person wielding the scalpel knew what he was doing. Maya stopped moving when she saw James approaching.

"How are you holding up?" he asked her, laying a hand on her shoulder.

"I'm alright." she said, forcing a smile. She would be better when Amy was safely out of surgery, but she didn't tell him that.

"How's Kyle?" she asked, changing the subject.

"They just finished stitching him up and he's been set up in a room down the hall. The doctors want him to spend the night, but he'll be fine." James explained.

"He's a tough kid." Maya said fondly and James nodded his agreement.

"Did he say anything about his father?" she asked curiously.

"He hasn't explained anything yet. He said he'll only talk to you." James told her and Maya smiled. She'd been trying to pry the information out of both teens for so long that it seemed fitting for Kyle to make sure that she got the information first.

"I'll wait here in case someone comes looking for you. You should go talk to him." James suggested and Maya nodded, turning to leave. She touched his arm lightly.

"Thanks." she said, looking up into his eyes. He just shook his head, waving her off with a tender smile.

Kyle was sitting up in bed, looking out the window when Maya walked in. He seemed surprised to see her and twisted his hands nervously in his lap when she pulled up a chair next to the bed.

"I'm really sorry about Amy. I should've done something to stop my dad from hurting her." Kyle rushed to say. Maya just shook her head and gazed at him sadly.

"It wasn't your fault Kyle. There is nothing you could have done." Maya said, trying to alleviate his guilt.

"My dad's the one who was hurting Amy, not our sensei. I asked her not to tell you, because I didn't want to get him in trouble. He's all I have…" Kyle said trailing off and looking like he might cry.

"It's alright Kyle."

"No, it's not alright. I shouldn't have asked Amy to lie to you. I never wanted to cause trouble for you, I was just scared. My dad's been doing drugs for a long time. He started making me buy drugs for him a few months ago. I knew he would hurt me if I didn't so I just did what I was told. Amy and I walked in when my dad and his friend were shooting up one night. They attacked us and my dad said that he would kill you and Amy if she told you. So we kept it a secret. I was saving my money and

I was going to run away when school was over. Amy was going to tell you everything once I was gone. But then she was attacked by that guy and you arrested our sensei-" Kyle explained, but Maya broke in, when she realized what he had said.

"She was attacked by who?" Maya asked, furrowing her brow.

"We went to school after Christmas to buy drugs one night. Amy stayed in the gym while I went to meet the drug dealer and some guy attacked her. He was trying to choke her, but I scared him off when I knocked over all the sports equipment. I told her she should tell you, but she didn't want to get me in trouble for buying drugs, so she kept it a secret. I'm really sorry, Maya." Kyle repeated, looking repentant.

"I know you are sweetie. Why don't you get some rest and we'll talk some more later?" Maya suggested as she leaned over and gave him a hug before turning to leave.

"Maya?" he called and she turned back around, looking at him questioningly.

"Will I go to jail?" he asked in a small voice, looking much younger than sixteen without his glasses, lying in the large hospital bed.

"Of course not! Why would you ask that?" Maya asked him, confused.

"I bought drugs. That's illegal and there are probably drugs in my house." Kyle explained, looking down at his hands.

"Have you ever taken drugs?" Maya asked, even though she already knew the answer to that question.

"No way!" Kyle said, looking horrified.

"That's what I thought. Your father put you in danger by making you buy drugs and by bringing drugs into the house. He abused you, he neglected you and he tried to kill you. Your father is going to jail Kyle. You didn't do anything wrong. You were just doing what you had to do to survive and I'm very proud of you for that. You handled yourself like a real man today. You stood up to your father and you risked your life to help Amy. And I love you for that." Maya said, having to choke out the last part as tears closed off her throat. Kyle's tears spilled over at that and Maya sat down on the edge of the bed and hugged him close, giving him a kiss on the head.

"I'll come back and check on you later." Maya said a few minutes later as she stood up and wiped away her tears. Kyle ducked his head and nodded, embarrassed to be crying in front of Amy's mother.

"Amy's going to be alright, isn't she?" he asked, seeming afraid to hear the answer.

"She should be fine. I'm just waiting for her to come out of surgery." Maya assured him and Kyle let his head fall back against the pillow, finally able to relax now that he had spilled his guts and was sure that his friend was okay. It had been the longest day ever and all Kyle wanted to do was sleep. He watched Maya leave and then let his eyes close. For once, he actually felt safe. He didn't know what would happen to him tomorrow, but he would worry about that then. For now, he was content and too tired to think about anything else.

☙

Thankfully, Amy came out of surgery all right and after spending a few hours in the recovery room, she was moved to Kyle's room. Maya sat in a chair between the two beds, half asleep. The sun was just rising when Amy finally woke up.

"Mom?" she said in a raspy voice and Maya's eyes shot open. She moved closer to the bed took her daughter's hand in her own.

"Hey" Maya said with a smile. Amy smiled back and squeezed her mother's hand lightly.

"How are you feeling?" Maya asked, her eyes glued to her daughter's face.

"Like I was shot." Amy joked in a voice barely above a whisper.

"Very funny." Maya said with a smirk and Amy's grin widened. Then she turned serious.

"Mom, it wasn't my sensei who was hurting me." Amy said, her eyes boring into her mother's.

"I know, Kyle told me everything." Maya assured her, reaching up to smooth Amy's hair away from her face.

"I'm sorry I lied to you. I hated it. It was really hard not to just tell you everything. You're not exactly an easy person to say no to." Amy said.

"Good, then maybe you won't do it so often." Maya tried, keeping the mood light.

"Oh mom!" Amy said, rolling her eyes.

"Seriously though, it was awful having you lie to me like that. I just hated knowing that you didn't trust me enough to tell me what was really going on. I don't care what kind of trouble you're in Amy, I will always help you. I don't ever want you to be afraid to tell me something." Maya said, making sure to hold Amy's gaze for her entire speech. When she was done, Amy ducked her head.

"I know. I just didn't want you to get in trouble at work. I didn't know what to do. You're not going to arrest Kyle are you?" Amy asked suddenly, the thought crossing her mind. She struggled to sit up in bed and Maya gently pushed her back down and moved to sit on the bed next to Amy.

"Calm down, Kyle's not going to get arrested. His father's the only one who's going to jail." Maya told her daughter, keeping her hands firmly on her daughter's shoulders. Tears filled Amy's eyes.

"He's an awful man, mom. He's always drugged up and he has these scary friends that are always over. He's mean and dangerous and he doesn't even buy food for Kyle. People like him shouldn't even be allowed to have kids!" Amy said forcefully.

"You're right, not everyone deserves to be a parent." Maya agreed, feeling her daughter's pain. She had come to care about Kyle a lot and the thought of him living like that just broke t. Although she and Ken were neighbors, she rarely saw him and she never went into his house. If she had known, she would have reported him for abuse and neglect a long time ago.

"Yeah, if only kids could choose their own parents. Then everything would be better." Amy said, staring across the room at Kyle's sleeping form. The longing in her voice squeezed Maya's chest and made it hard for her to breathe. Andrew's words came back to her and she knew she had to find out if he was right.

"If you could pick your own parents, what would they be like?" Maya asked, trying to sound casual as she made herself more comfortable. Amy looked at her as if she had suddenly grown a second head. When Maya waited expectantly, Amy looked down at the blanket partially covering her.

"I would pick you, but with a nice husband. Someone funny and really nice who loved us and would take us to baseball games and teach me how to play sports and ride my bike. We would go fishing and camping and not have to cancel all the time for work, because his family would be more important. He would drop us off at the mall and then roll his eyes when he saw all the crap we bought when he came to pick us up. Like the families in the Disney movies. It's corny, I know. Must be the drugs talking." Amy said, her cheeks reddening in embarrassment.

"So what you're really saying is that you wish I wouldn't work so much so that we could spend more time together and you hate Harry." Maya said, slowly. She watched as Amy's cheeks reddened even more and she started to squirm.

"That's not what I said." she protested, but Maya cut her off with a wave.

"It's what you meant and you're right. I do work too much. It's not right for us to go days without seeing each other. And I can't even remember the last time we went shopping or spent any time together that didn't involve eating." Maya told her daughter and Amy glanced up at her.

"Me either." she said softly.

"I will do my best to change that. I can't help the fact that I have to work, but I can arrange my time better. What I don't understand though, is what you could possibly have against Harry, since you barely even know him." Maya said, looking puzzled. Amy rolled her eyes and smirked.

"Trust me, you don't want to know." she said bitterly.

"Tell me." her mother insisted and Amy shrugged.

"Your James Bond tried to bribe me." Amy said casually.

"He did what?" Maya asked incredulously.

"He wanted to pay me to make sure that I told you I liked him. Don't worry, I didn't take his money." Amy explained and her mother looked disgusted.

"What an Ass! I can't believe he did that!" Maya exclaimed standing and holding her hands up.

"My thoughts exactly." Amy agreed and Maya shook her head.

"Why didn't you tell me this before?" Maya asked with a frown as she stood beside the hospital bed with her hands on her hips.

"You liked him. I didn't want to be the one to ruin your new relationship." Amy said with a shrug.

"So you were going to let me find out on my own that he was a jerk?" Maya asked, raising one eyebrow. Amy laughed as she realized what her mother was saying.

"Okay, so maybe that was slightly stupid. I probably should've told you." Amy conceded and Maya sat back down on her daughter's bed.

"There's something else you should've told me." Maya hinted seriously and Amy hung her head.

"Who attacked you at school Amy?"

"I don't know who he was. I was in the gym and he just grabbed me from behind. He grabbed my arm and I thought he was going to snap my elbow, but I twisted with him so it didn't hurt so much. He tried to hit me in the face, but I blocked it that's why my face was so scratched up. Then he went for my neck and started choking me. I thought I was going to die, but then Kyle made all that noise and scared him away. I was really scared. I wanted to tell you, but I couldn't exactly tell you that we were buying drugs." Amy explained, but Maya wasn't listening anymore. She was too busy thinking, trying to figure it all out.

"What did he look like?" she asked her daughter absently.

"It was really dark, so I didn't get a good look. I know he was taller than me and he was really strong. I think he had dark hair that was cut really short... I really don't know mom." Amy said, getting frustrated when she couldn't quite picture the man.

"It's all right, honey. Do you think you would recognize him if you saw him again?" Maya asked gently, trying not to upset her daughter.

"I guess." Amy answered, looking a little frightened at the thought.

"You don't have to worry. Now that I know what's going on, I'm not going to let anyone near you." Maya promised, stroking her daughter's hair lightly.

"I know." Amy said, showing more confidence in her mother than Maya had in herself.

"I love you. I don't know what I would have done if..." Maya trailed off, unable to say the words out loud. She wasn't usually this open with Amy, but seeing her daughter almost bleed to death in front of her had really opened her eyes to what was important. She saw Amy's eyes start to droop and Maya leaned forward and kissed her daughter's forehead.

"You should get some rest." she said and Amy nodded, but when Maya went to leave the room her eyes opened wide.

"You're leaving?" Amy asked, in a small voice.

"I'm just going to talk to James, I won't be long." Maya promised and Amy settled back into the pillows, letting her eyes close. Maya took a moment to just look at her daughter and she thanked God for the hundredth time for saving her baby girl.

Chapter 12

"You're sure?" their Captain asked Maya and James when Maya finished explaining what Amy had told them.

"Yes, I'm sure. It's the same M.O. and the guy that Amy described fits the description from the other two girls." Maya explained.

"Which wasn't much." her captain reminded her.

"I know, but Amy thinks she can recognize him if she sees him again. We have to get him before he hurts someone else." Maya said. *And I want him punished for what he did to my little girl*, she finished silently.

"So you want to set up a trap. You better be damn sure that you have all your bases covered before you set out your bait. I don't want another girl hurt because our department is incompetent." the captain pressured and Maya and James nodded vehemently.

"Yes sir. We'll have all exits covered and eyes on the girl at all times. We'll dot all the Is and cross all the Ts." James assured him. The captain inclined his head briefly in what could have been a half-hearted attempt at a nod and then marched out of the hospital waiting room.

"Now we just need to find someone to use as bait and get the team together. We'll get this bastard yet." James said, pounding his fist into his other hand.

"You'll have to do all that without me. I've got more pressing problems at the moment." Maya said wearily.

"Care to elaborate?" James asked with a frown.

"Both kids are being released today and I've got to convince social services to let Kyle come home with me." Maya said, leaning back against the wall and crossing her arms over her chest. James' frown transformed into a broad grin. He placed both hands on Maya's cheeks and then planted a kiss on her lips. Maya blinked in surprise when he leaned back a smile splitting his face and something more in his eyes.

"What was that for?" she sputtered, totally caught off guard by his show of affection.

"You really are amazing. Kyle is going to be ecstatic when you tell him. He's wanted to be a part of your family for a very long time." James said, never taking his eyes off Maya's.

"How would you know?" she asked, feeling like she was missing something.

"It's written all over his face every time you guys are together." James explained, with a knowing look. Maya closed her eyes and shook her head in disbelief. His words surprised her, but not nearly as much as his kiss had. She raised a hand to her lips involuntarily and then yanked it away. They were friends and nothing more. James was just very happy that she was going to fight for Kyle.

"Well it's not going to be easy to convince them that I'm the best person for the job. I work up to a hundred hours a week and I live in a two bedroom apartment. Not to mention the fact that my own daughter was just shot. Oh and the fact that the kids were buying drugs and I never suspected a thing." Maya said, trying to take the focus away from his compliment. She never had been very good at taking compliments.

"It's not like they were using the drugs, besides social services would be stupid to turn you down. Kyle wouldn't stay with anyone else." James assured her and then pulled out his cell phone.

"Give Amy a kiss for me. Tell them I'll stop by the apartment later. Now I've gotta run if I'm going to get everything set up for tomorrow." James added and waved to Maya as he left the waiting room.

♥

Amy struggled with her crutches as she tried to get to her feet. Kyle just watched from his hospital bed where he sat dressed in a new sweater and jeans that Maya had bought him. A woman from social services had come by to talk to him earlier. She kept asking questions about his family, mostly about his mother. The lady didn't seem to believe him when he said that he had no idea where she was and that he didn't care. Now he just waited to see where they were going to send him. He figured it would probably be a group home. He just hoped that it would be somewhere close by so that he could still hang out with Amy and go to the same school.

"Are you ready? We have to hurry because I left my car parked in a no parking zone right next to the front door. Here, let me help you." Maya said breezing into the room and helping Amy get her balance on the crutches. Kyle watched helplessly as they started for the door. He wanted so badly to follow them that his legs twitched in anticipation. Amy was almost around the corner when she turned to look at him.

"Kyle." she called him and then lost her balance. She whacked her mother in the shins with one of her crutches and Maya swore under her breath as she grabbed Amy around the waist to keep her from falling over. When they had once again started moving, Maya turned back to Kyle and saw that he was sitting on his bed watching them.

"Didn't you hear me, Kyle? Move your butt before I get a parking ticket. Then James will laugh at me for a week." Maya said and Kyle looked at her hopefully, his mouth dropping open. The women disappeared around the corner and Kyle stood up, uncertain as to what to do.

"If you don't hurry up, you're going to have to run behind the car!" he heard Maya say from the hallway. Kyle lurched forward and broke into a run, having trouble seeing where he was going around the happy tears in his eyes and the smile that was so wide it was making him squint. He caught up to them in two seconds flat and Maya smiled at him, putting her arm around his shoulders.

"You didn't really think I was going to leave you here did you?" she asked teasingly. Kyle couldn't talk around the lump in his throat. He felt Maya kiss him on the cheek, before releasing him and helping Amy into the elevator.

"You're blushing, Kyle." Amy pointed out, laughing at him. Maya smiled and her eyes twinkled as she gazed at him with an amused look on her face. Kyle just shrugged. Nothing anyone could say could make his smile disappear because he was finally getting what he had always wanted.

෴

James did stop by that night. Amy was resting on the couch, while she and Kyle watched TV and bickered as if they had been brother and sister all their lives. James bent to kiss Amy on the cheek and she smiled up at him happily. She looked so relaxed and content that James just wanted to sit next to her and forget everything else that was going on. Instead, he went over to Kyle and punched him playfully in the shoulder.

"How are you holding up, buddy?" he asked, perching on the arm of the easy chair where Kyle was sitting.

"I'm good." Kyle answered, looking up briefly. Maya walked into the room and Kyle smiled at her, his eyes lighting up. James chuckled and winked at Maya. She just rolled her eyes at him and he ruffled Kyle's hair as he got back to his feet. Kyle ducked away from his hand and squinted his eyes menacingly. James held up his hands in surrender and tried not to laugh.

"I know, I know. Don't mess with the tough guy." James said, only half joking.

"That's right! Don't you forget it!" Kyle said, puffing out his chest and flexing his muscles. Amy burst out laughing and Maya bit back a smile.

"You proved how tough you are yesterday Kyle. We'll never forget it." James said more seriously. Kyle blushed, but he looked pleased. James gave him one last smile before turning away. He walked towards Maya who looked at him questioningly. He stopped in front of her and pulled her to her feet, taking hold of her elbow and guiding her towards the kitchen. Maya leaned against the counter, while James stood in front of her.

"Do you think she'll be ready for tomorrow?" he asked Maya and she frowned.

"Who?" she asked, although deep down she knew what he meant.

"Amy. We need her to identify her attacker. You know that." James said, looking at Maya strangely. Maya felt queasy at the thought of taking her daughter anywhere near that monster.

"She's still weak and on painkillers. I don't know…" Maya said non-commitally.

"We don't have a choice, Maya. She's the only one who can identify him." James coaxed, but Maya was still reluctant to put Amy in that situation.

"What about Vanessa or Allison?" Maya tried, but James shook his head.

"Vanessa didn't see his face and Allison is still in the hospital. Come on Maya, you know the drill. What are you so anxious about?" James asked, looking deep into her eyes. Maya squirmed under his intense gaze and felt like he could see right through her.

"She's my baby James and I almost lost her. I just…" Maya trailed off, unable to explain to him how she really felt.

"You'll be right there with her. He won't get anywhere near her. We'll make sure of that." James said reassuringly. Maya didn't say anything as she struggled to convince herself. She knew that what he was saying was true. She had said the same things hundreds of times to victims and their families. But now her daughter was the victim and everything had changed. She wasn't sure of anything anymore. She felt this primal instinct to protect Amy that she had never felt this strong before. James stayed silent as she wrestled with herself.

"The fact that your daughter was shot doesn't make you a bad mother, Maya. You saved her life." Maya swallowed against the lump that had suddenly appeared in her throat as her friend seemed to read her mind. James stepped closer and took her hands in his. Maya looked up at him, searching his eyes.

"She's lucky to have you. We all are." James said and Maya was about to look away when James caught her lips in a sweet kiss. She was less surprised this time and closed her eyes savoring the moment. She let all her worries go as her arms wrapped around his neck. For just a minute, she let herself feel.

❧

"Amy, come here!" Kyle whispered forcefully. Amy dragged herself to the doorway and together they peeked into the kitchen. Kyle looked excitedly at Amy and she couldn't help but smile as she took in the scene. They watched with excitement as James and Maya kissed. Amy and Kyle had both wanted them to get together for more than two years. Kyle turned away from the scene long enough to pump his fist in the air.

"Yessss!" he hissed and Amy clamped a hand over her mouth to keep from laughing out loud. She felt giddy and happy. Everything finally seemed to be going right. She had come clean with her mother, Kyle was coming to live with them and Maya and James finally seemed to be hooking up, which meant no more Harry. Amy couldn't be happier. She let a giggle escape as she slapped Kyle's raised hand in a high five. Maya quickly pulled away at the sound and stared at the teens. She shared a look with James and then stepped away from him and strode quickly towards Kyle and Amy.

"Ooouuu, mooom!" Amy said, dragging out the syllables to tease her mother.

"All right, all right. Show's over. Now get back on that couch, you're not supposed to be on your feet." Maya admonished, not quite looking either teen in the eyes. She got Amy settled back on the couch and then sat down next to her, while Kyle plopped down on the floor in front of them. James joined Kyle on the floor, acting like nothing had happened. Kyle glanced at Amy over his shoulders with an amused expression on his face and Amy burst out laughing.

༄

She wasn't laughing the next day, however, when she sat in the passenger seat of a department issue car next to her mother. They were stationed on the outskirts of the park, in an open area where they could see everything that was going on. It was a beautiful sunny day and people milled about everywhere in the park, walking, jogging or just enjoying the fresh air. The sun reflected off the snow and Amy had to shield her eyes as she nervously scanned the park for any sign of him. She could see a young girl doing what looked like yoga or Tai Chi in the snow on the far side of the park near some bushes. A familiar looking male jogger ran by for what was probably the fifth time, steam escaping his mouth with each breath, and the woman walking her dog stopped near a tree and glanced over at the girl. Another cop was hidden in the bushes out of sight and Amy knew that James was near the entrance of the high school that was situated at the opposite end of the park. They had all been there for more than an hour and Amy hadn't seen anyone that remotely resembled the monster in her memories. She was beginning to think that what she remembered wasn't very accurate. Maya sat next to her in silence, watching patiently out the window.

"What if he doesn't come?" Amy asked a few minutes later. Maya ignored her and leaned forward to peer more carefully at the yoga girl. A man had walked up to her and appeared to be hassling her.

"I don't think that's him." Amy said, when her mother looked at her questioningly. The man looked older and had a beard. His winter coat was brown, but Amy wasn't sure if that was the actual color or if it was just dirty. His sweat pants were tucked into his work boots and his neon orange toque stood a good six inches off the top of his head. Maya reached for the door handle as she watched the exchange. When the man grabbed the girl's wrist, Maya pushed open the door and leaped out of the car, hurrying over. Amy opened her door and got out of the car. Leaning on the hood for support, she watched as Maya and the jogger-cop approached them, guns raised. When the man released the girl and stepped away with his hands in the air, Amy got a good look at him and she knew that he wasn't the right guy. She was so enthralled in what was happening that she didn't even hear the footsteps. When she finally sensed his presence, it was too late to do anything about it. She felt his hand clamp over her mouth to effectively muffle her scream and his other arm snaked around her middle. He picked her up effortlessly and started to back away from the car.

"You were never supposed to live. Mistakes can not be forgiven. If it's not perfection it's not good enough. So now I'm going to fix my mistake." he said, his voice sounding low and gravelly. Amy struggled in is grasp and kicked her legs, wincing when she felt the wound in her leg open up, the stitches ripped. He dragged her behind some trees and Amy was again surprised at his strength. She couldn't believe this was happening again. When her mother had told her that she would have to help with the investigation, Amy had balked, afraid that something like this would happen. Now she closed her eyes and waited for him to finish her off. Time seemed to stand still as Amy waited to die.

"Amy!" she heard and her eyes snapped open. Her mother was running towards them. Amy felt the man stop and he put her down, his arm wrapping around her chest and shoulders, while his other hand grabbed the side of her head. Maya slowed to a walk and raised her gun.

"Let her go!" she yelled, breathing hard. Amy could see her mother waver as she found herself pointing her gun at Amy.

"Drop the gun or I break her neck. You know I can do it." the man said over Amy's head, sounding perfectly calm. Maya ignored him for a moment, pointing the gun at his head before slowly lowering it and tossing it into the snow a few feet away.

"Okay, now just let her go and we can work something out." Maya bargained for the second time in three days. The man threw back his head and laughed, momentarily loosening his grip on Amy. Seizing the opportunity, Amy stomped hard on his foot and cranked her elbow back as hard as she could, catching him in the gut. When he doubled over in pain, she threw her head back, knocking him in the face. She heard him groan and heard the snow crunching as her mother ran towards them. Amy tried to get away, but he held on firmly to her arm.

"I told you to let her go!" Maya growled as she swung at him, her punch getting him square in the face, making his head snap back. He finally released Amy and she stumbled forward, falling into the cold, wet snow. By the time she looked back, Maya had wrenched his arm behind his back and was trying to cuff him. With a deft move, he kicked his leg back, sweeping Maya off her feet. He was about to hit her when James jumped him from behind. Amy hadn't even seen him run up. James wrestled the man to the ground, using brute strength to try to subdue him. He used another move to flip himself over until he was on top of James. He punched James in the face hard twice while Amy screamed. By then, Maya was back on her feet and she kicked him hard. She kicked him over and over, until he finally lay still on the ground, moaning.

"That's enough, Maya." James said, grabbing Maya by the shoulders and turning her around. Amy thought for a moment that she was going to hit him, but instead she seemed to dissolve into him and James pulled her close. The jogger-cop managed to snap handcuffs onto the attacker, while the dog-walker spoke into her radio. Maya let James hold her for a moment while she cried and then she broke away. She ran over to Amy and dropped to her knees in front of her daughter, putting her arms around Amy. Amy could feel her mother's heart pounding and she realized that Maya had been just as scared as she herself had been. Amy hugged her mother back tightly and sighed. It was finally over.

"That was definitely him." she said and her mother laughed through her tears.

"God I hope so!" Maya exclaimed, smiling shakily. She got up and then pulled Amy to her feet, slipping her arm around her daughter's waist to support her. With her free hand, she wiped away tears from Amy's cheeks that she hadn't even realized she had cried. Then Maya kissed Amy's forehead and forced a smile.

"Let's go home."

❦

Maya drove Amy and Kyle back to karate a week later. She had already apologized to Greg Boltis for arresting him and now it was Kyle and Amy's turn. Kyle led the way while Amy hobbled awkwardly on her crutches. She had torn all her stitches when she struggled to get away from her attacker and was now forced to stay off the leg even longer. They waited until class was over and then they approached their sensei.

"It's good to see you guys. I'm glad you're both alright." he said sincerely and Kyle felt even more guilty.

"We just wanted to say that we're really sorry for all the trouble we caused. We didn't mean for any of it to happen." Amy said, acting as spokesperson.

"I know. I understand why you did it, but getting charged for a crime like that is not something I take lightly." he said and Kyle hung his head.

"My mom thought it was you who was hurting me because I kept telling her that I got the bruises at karate. I never thought she would arrest you." Amy explained.

"Yeah and we didn't know that it was the killer who attacked Amy, otherwise we would have said something sooner." Kyle added.

"So how did your mom get so messed up in her investigation anyways?" Sensei asked, crossing his arms.

"She was actually on the right track. The killer has a black belt in karate but he hasn't trained formally in years. He was a gymnastics coach and agent for really advanced gymnasts. Apparently, his best athlete was killed in a car accident a few years ago. She was supposed to go to the Olympics and he kind of lost it when she died. So he started researching other athletes and eventually killed the ones who quit. He thought it was unfair that they were alive and they were throwing away their talent, while his athlete died. So he was punishing them. Eventually, he just needed the high that he got from the attacks and that's why he attacked girls like me." Amy explained, her voice strong until the end. It still bothered her that she had come that close to death three times in as many weeks.

"Thanks for coming by to explain. I don't hold any of this against you guys. I promise I won't beat you up, as long as you come back to class as soon as you're ready." Sensei said seriously. The teens looked at each other, unsure. Kyle knew that Amy wasn't planning on returning to karate and he wasn't sure that he would come back either. Their sensei seemed to sense this and he continued.

"You shouldn't be afraid to come back. Not all black belts are like him. Karate is not about violence, it's about getting to know yourself so that fighting becomes one of many tools available if there comes a time when you have to use it."

☙

They walked hand in hand amidst the crowd. People were everywhere, bumping into them and talking loudly. Some were singing, the music lingering even though the concert was long since over. Others were talking excitedly about their experience, hoping to immortalize the night with pictures and souvenirs. Amy and Kyle hurried back after having each purchased a T-shirt. Their gleeful expressions and their starry eyes were a testament to the success of the night out. James held Maya's hand tightly and leaned over to kiss her teasingly. She smiled wider as he pulled back and gave his full attention to the kids.

"Look what we got! Aren't they awesome?" Amy asked bounding over to her mother's side.

"Very cool." Maya agreed, slipping an arm around her daughter's waist. She had finally come to realize that Amy wasn't nearly as embarrassed by this type of show of affection as Maya had originally thought. The hands-off policy that they had once entertained seemed stupid now. Maya felt completely natural, walking with her boyfriend and two kids, looking like part of a family instead of the independent woman that she had always strived to be. Kyle unrolled the poster he had tucked under his arm and showed it to James. James nodded approvingly and Kyle's grin lit up his face. He was starting to look less gaunt and he really felt comfortable in his new home environment. He just couldn't wait to put the poster up his new room. Their apartment suddenly too small, Maya had moved them to a bigger apartment nearby, which just happened to be very near to James' place. They were already planning a camping trip for the four of them when Kyle and Amy got out of school. James absolutely wanted to teach the teens how to fly fish and they were both very excited about it.

"So are you going to come?" Kyle was asking and Maya forced herself to pay attention to what he was saying.

"I don't know if your sensei would be very happy to see us there." James said slowly.

"It's the most important tournament of the year! You've got to come! Besides, Sensei said that he wasn't mad at you. He said that he totally understood why you did it. Please, say you'll come." Amy begged, pleading with her eyes. Since Amy rarely asked for anything, Maya figured this must be really important to her.

"Of course we'll come, won't we James?" Maya answered, looking up at him and daring him to contradict her.

"Sure. I know better than to argue with your mom once she's made up her mind." James added under his breath to Kyle. Kyle grinned and ducked his head. Amy giggled like a child, momentarily leaving behind the adult she had been forced to grow up into recently.

"Yeah and Sensei Charles said that maybe this year we can win the cup. Anyone who wins a medal gets points and they're going to add up all the points for each club. Our club has never won the cup before." Kyle explained and James put his hand on the nape of Kyle's neck and squeezed lightly.

"Well I guess you guys are gonna have to change that." he said and the teens nodded vigorously.

"Yep. We want to win." Amy answered and Maya looked over at her daughter.

"Just try not to get your nose broken. Your birthday's coming up and I want at least one set of pictures where your face isn't black and blue." Maya told her and Amy laughed.

"Sure mom." she said and Kyle glanced at her thoughtfully.

"What do you want for your birthday this year, Amy?" he asked as they walked across the parking lot, nearing Maya's car. She always insisted on driving, even though James thought it would be more gentlemanly for him to be the one driving. Maya climbed into the driver's seat and Amy got in behind her. James slid into the passenger seat without complaining and fastened his seat belt.

"Well?" Kyle prompted, doing the same.

"Something borrowed and something blue." Amy answered, cryptically.

"Huh?" Kyle said, looking confused. Maya caught her daughter's eye in the rear view mirror.

"We'll see." was all she said as she backed out of the parking spot.

"And a sword. The *Shihan* is going to teach us *Iaido* next time he comes to visit. That's the art of sword drawing. He's going to show us how to draw out the sword and slice our opponent right down the middle. Doesn't that sound super cool?" Amy asked and Maya felt herself shudder at the vision her daughter had conjured up. Just when she was starting to get used to Amy getting banged up at karate, her daughter wanted to play with long sharp objects. Great. Just great.

"I should've had a boy." Maya mumbled and James snickered beside her. She punched him playfully as Amy leaned forward in her seat.

"But then everyone would tell you that your son hits like a girl." Amy protested and Kyle laughed while James rubbed his arm. He twisted in his seat so that he was facing Amy, still holding his arm and spoke to her seriously.

"Trust me, that is not a bad thing."

About the Author

Stéphanie Julien is a recent graduate of Laurentian University with an honours degree in Biomedical Biology. She has a brown belt in karate and has enjoyed reading and writing for most of her life. This is her first novel.

Printed in the United States
93239LV00001B/10-108/A